FUTURE X

PRAISE for **FUTURE X** *by Georg Koszulinski*

"*FUTURE X* is a bold and timely work. It is an honest and unflinching confrontation with much of what's wrong with our shared culture. . . Koszulinski's vision of madness, at once apocalyptic and dystopian, challenges readers to honestly assess their situation, and consider how we might live more modestly together in prosperity and peace, without resorting to genocide or war on civilians."
—Paul Hunter, author of the award-winning book *Breaking Ground*

"In *FUTURE X*, award-winning filmmaker and now award-winning novelist Georg Koszulinski gives the reader a timely mash-up of national and ecological collapse, pandemic, and technological dystopia narratives to explore the most dangerous, large-scale, anthropogenic variants ('x') of our possible futures.

"The central drama is one of transmission: the story revolves around an ex-marine who wanders a post-apocalyptic landscape in search of other survivors and happens upon the Dead Man's writings, which are part media and narrative theory, part descriptions of his work in 'archeopsychic extractions.' The protagonist Jane Ballard and a small group of survivors receive a radio message broadcast from the southern hemisphere from others who have likewise made it through multiple overlapping extinction events. And we, the readers, are receiving Jane's transmission in a twenty-second-century future defined by the historical events she lived through and also the conditions today for the transmission of information and disinformation, knowledge and viral stupidity, and wisdom and world-crashing data.

"Appropriately, *FUTURE X* explores a mash-up of genres best suited to engage realistically and speculatively the challenges of storytelling at a time of the nonhuman turn and species-level existential danger: the expository mode, journal entry, memoir, notes, encyclopedia preface, court document, historiographic timeline, and aphorism. At this moment in history, Koszulinski's novel brings together all the X's influencing what the Dead Man describes as 'our collective failure to imagine our way out of this world and into another.'"
—Charles M. Tung, author of *Modernism and Time Machines*

"Kozulinski's debut novel is timely, masterful, and raw. Set in a nightmarish future, it is a visionary tale of survival and self-discovery in a world ravaged by the climate crisis, AI, and unchecked capitalism."
—Pavithra Tantrigoda, Professor of English, University of Central Florida

FUTURE X

Georg Koszulinski

RAVEN
CHRONICLES PRESS
Shoreline/Seattle, Washington

RAVEN
CHRONICLES PRESS

Printed in the United States of America

Print ISBN: 979-8-9914032-1-4
eBook ISBN: 979-8-9914032-2-1
Library of Congress Control Number: 2025932110

FUTURE X is a work of fiction. Names, characters, places, and incidents are the product of the author's imagination or are used fictitiously. Any resemblance to actual events, locals, or persons, living or dead, is entirely coincidental.

Library of Congress Cataloging-in-Publication Data:
Koszulinski, Georg, 1979.
  FUTURE X: a work of speculative fiction / by Georg Koszulinski.

Cover artwork: *Untitled*, video glitch image, Josh Yates, 2025.
Book Design: Phoebe Bosché, using Adobe Jenson Pro (text), and
    Proxima Nova (display).
Cover Design: Scott Martin.
Author's photo on back cover: by Renee Cranford

Raven Chronicles Press
15528 12th Avenue N.E.
Shoreline, Washington 98155-6226
https://www.ravenchronicles.org

Contents

FOREWORD

Why do people read literature, especially fiction? To live other lives, to feel and more fully savor their own existence. To entertain and learn from alternatives to the lives they awoke to, maybe chose or were forced into, but eventually accepted as their lot, if not their fate. We all wish to grow in understanding and purpose, to feel a kinship with nature and a freedom beyond the confines of the everyday.

In the case of Georg Koszulinski's *FUTURE X*, the reader may crave to avoid living a life like those warped, damaged, and ended by a human society whose technology and values have run amok. This prize-winning dystopian novel imagines the failure of the human experience in a future that is uncomfortably near, with clues to our possible undoing at the moment all around. The main character and narrator is a Black ex-Marine woman named Jane Ballard, who spends years searching for another living soul in the deserts of the American Southwest, before she happens upon Dead Man, a desiccated corpse with his knapsack of writings, canned hams, and bottled water. And there she finds a purpose—carrying on Dead Man's unfinished story, telling what happened to humanity in its final struggles, as best she can. Her own sins are part of the story, and she tells us there is almost no one innocent of wrongdoing by the end.

Her conflicted narrative is blunt, vulgar, baffled, and nearly always angry. Where is there to go with such a story of the end, and what is there to be done? Jane Ballard has health and energy to go with that fierce Marine training, but also guilt and despair. She doesn't want to raise monuments to the fallen, and never thinks for a moment of having a child of her own. But she also never quits for a moment imagining that she is not alone, that there must be survivors like Dead Man out there somewhere, who can start over and make a modest success given what she has written, these indelible lessons in what to avoid, and how to carry on.

Georg Koszulinski's novel *FUTURE X* speaks honestly to this moment of naked public greed, angry dismantling of government institutions, and denial of the obvious in a power grab that is unprecedented in our history. What remains to be done must begin with a stirring of will and a clear-eyed understanding of what is at stake—which is precisely the gift Koszulinski's book offers us.

—Paul Hunter
Keepers of the Fire Award, Fiction Judge

We all have the same thought.

Hope is the currency of the powerless.

They who control language control perception.

The past is rewritten at the future's expense.

Authenticity is a social construct.

The future is heresy.

PROLOGUE

LAST ENTRY

LISTEN, I HAVE TO STOP DOING THIS, recording my thoughts. It's an endless void, everyone knows that. I'm not going to find an ending to this, no such thing as endings, not even in true stories, just places where we stop telling you what happened or get tired of keeping account or trick ourselves into thinking there's a satisfactory place to stop. There isn't.

I've lost so many notes over the past decade, kept writing them down but the notebooks kept multiplying and I'm tired of trying to make sense of them. This is all out of order and out of control on so many levels and I'm in no state to go back and make sense of any of this. In fits of depression or rage I threw my notes down the cliffsides, burned them, or just abandoned them when we left Taos. Maybe you can find the rest of my rants from the place out west we used to call home, but why would you want to do that? I almost took this entire stack of papers and threw them off the side of the ship, thinking maybe it was the writing that was poisoning my mind, but realized that wouldn't solve any of my problems.

But these notes are a record of my time. They'll outlive me and that's got to count for something. I'm suppressing the urge to write FUCK YOU in large letters right now. If you're reading this then it's not the worst of all possible endings, is it?

If there's a moral to this story it's don't let the dead into your head. They'll never leave because you have the one thing they want and are never going to get. It's like the saying over every Californian immigrant cemetery. *Was du bist, das waren wir; was wir sind, das wirst du sein / What you are, that is what we were. What we are, that is what you will be.*

It's the sound of ice scraping against the hull. It's the engine of despair inside my stomach, a new kind of fear I've not felt before. It's thinking fondly of being buried in the ground. Dying at sea is like being erased from history. It's like never having existed in the first place. My mouth tastes like chalk. It's a privilege to be buried. Trust me on that one. *We were once you.* It will be fine. It's built to endure this. *And you will be us.*

Words are a weapon. Words sink to the bottom where they live forever. Maybe it's the sound a Dusky Seaside Sparrow makes, or of my own short breaths, which I cannot hear only feel in my cinched-up chest, snuffed out by the drone of this ship. *Oohhhhhmmmm.* Don't let the dead in your head. Don't let the dead in your head. Don't let the dead—

Also, and I'm sorry to have to tell you this, but there's the ghost of an extinct bird on this ship.

PREFATORY NOTE, *WORLD BOOK ENCYCLOPEDIA*, 1979 EDITION

WORLD BOOK ENCYCLOPEDIA *is a tool for learning—a general encyclopedia that tells about people, places, things, events, and ideas. It provides accurate information that is easy to understand.*

You may come to your encyclopedia for the answer to a particular question, such as "How high is a badminton net?" or "What is the population of Haiti?" Or you may seek general information for a school assignment. Parents and young people, when they plan together for the future, often come to the World Book Encyclopedia to find out about the possibilities in various careers. And, of course, many people like simply to explore World Book Encyclopedia, *letting one topic lead to another. Browsing or skimming through the encyclopedia is an enjoyable way to pick up interesting information on many subjects.*

All articles, generally called entries, are arranged alphabetically, volume by volume and subject by subject. Included in this alphabetical arrangement are also thousands of entry cross-references.

The alphabetical system used in the World Book Encyclopedia *is the same system used in arranging a telephone directory and the card catalogs of books in most libraries. In most instances,* World Book Encyclopedia's *alphabetical arrangement of articles and cross-references will enable you to find the information you are seeking.*

A note on the revision program: an encyclopedia must be up to date if it is to serve the best interests of its users. A revised edition of World Book Encyclopedia *is published each year. Each edition reflects up-to-date information and the latest changes in educational viewpoints. Every subject area is under continuing surveillance. The annual revision program is never confined to a single area or to certain volumes. Thousands of pages are revised or updated each year.*

UNITED STATES OF AMERICA V. UNPRIVILEGED BELLIGERENTS

and their Agents, "The California Republic Armed Forces," heretofore referred to as "the paramilitary organization." United States District Court for the Western District of Missouri.

Indictment: Unprivileged Belligerency
This indictment charges all members concurrently and without prejudice, 'the paramilitary organization,' with violations of federal law, specifically related to acts of unprivileged belligerency. The charges are brought under the authority of the United States Code, Title 18, Sections 2331 and 2339A.
Count 1: Providing material support to paramilitary groups (18 U.S.C. § 2339A).
Count 2: Conspiracy to provide material support to paramilitary groups (18 U.S.C. § 2339B).
Count 3: Using and carrying firearms during and in relation to crimes of violence against Federal agents, U.S. military personnel, and non-combatant civilians (18 U.S.C. § 924©(1)(A)).
Count 4: Treason. 18 U.S. Code § 2381, anyone who, owing allegiance to the United States, levies war against them or adheres to their enemies, giving them aid and comfort, is guilty of treason. The penalty for treason is death.

This court has jurisdiction over this matter pursuant to 18 U.S.C. § 3231. The offenses were committed within the jurisdiction of the United States and its territories.

Defendants
The defendants are identified as members of the unlawful paramilitary organization and their affiliates. Individuals include all citizens of the United States who have renounced their citizenship, taken up arms against the U.S. Military, or provided material aid or comfort to the enemy, the paramilitary organization, and its affiliates.

Offense Description

The defendants have or continue to engage in acts of unprivileged belligerency by providing material support, services, or aid and comfort to the paramilitary organization and its members. These actions include training, armed combat, espionage, conspiracy, and logistical support.

Legal Basis

Supplying services to the paramilitary organization in violation of Executive Order 13129 and 50 U.S.C. § 1705(b). Using and carrying firearms and destructive devices during crimes of violence in violation of 18 U.S.C. § 924©(1)(A). Providing material support to terrorist organizations under 18 U.S.C. § 2339A. Violations of 18 U.S. Code § 641: Public money, property or records. Violations of 18 U.S. Code § 2383: Rebellion or insurrection. Violations of 18 U.S. Code § 2384: Seditious conspiracy. Violations of U.S. Code § 272: Use of military equipment and facilities.

Forfeiture Allegation

Pursuant to 18 U.S.C. § 981(a)(1)(G), all assets derived from or used in the commission of the offenses are subject to forfeiture. The defendants are hereby charged with the offenses, and the United States of America seeks all appropriate legal remedies, including imprisonment, fines, forfeiture of assets, and death.

TIMELINE

2050s: Machine intelligence and the feed rise to global prominence

2055: I was born in Los Angeles, California

2059: First private colony established on the Moon

2064: Mexico-California alliance established

2068: My family moved to Grizzly Flats, California

2069: First material missions to Mars, Apollo Moon Landing Centennial

2071: First manned missions to Mars, colony established at
Valles Marineris

2072-73: Global famine, millions die in Africa, China, Europe,
Middle East

2073: Californian War of Independence, 15 states secede from
the Union

2074: I enlisted in the California Republic Marine Corps

2076: California-U.S. conflict comes to an end

2078-79: Global collapse

2085-86: Virus (x)

2087: The year I started taking notes about bird migrations

2091: The year I began writing in earnest

2101: Notes from the *Nerrivik*

Hope is for the oppressed.

Fear lubricates the engines of despair.

The weight of history is a murder weapon.

Peace is not merely the absence of war.

Security is a gilded cage.

PART 1

WINTER '91

Call me Jane. Contrary to popular belief, speaking in the first person is a sign of humility. All I have to offer is myself. Jane Ballard. Survived. Whatever happens, remember my name, it's all I have in this world. Like that long-ass and completely unreadable book about whales and going to sea, and the peril that it brought everyone on that ship, the story of my life follows a similar trajectory, which is better than I can say for everyone else.

I'll say from the start I'm in search of a more hopeful ending, a reclamation of my mind and some semblance of peace, just to breathe again. These words are what remain of my life, and I'd like each one to count for something. I'm warning you now that if this account of my life gets done, I get to some kind of ending, it's not going to make sense, get tied up, resolved, satisfactorily explained. It's not going to be like those old-world stories with tidied up beginnings, middles, and ends.

I'm writing this in the late winter of '91. The desert primrose and creosotes are starting to bloom. After spending the last few years riding my father's single-cylinder 125cc dirt bike up and down the coast, and once the remaining fuel reserves turned bad, zigzagging on a ten-speed across California, California in search of survivors, I decided to head east if for no other reason than I wanted to see the desert again, see if the place would help quiet my mind. Ask the dust.

The desert is the closest thing to magic I know of. It wields that kind of power, tricks you with its beauty. It's also actively trying to kill you, sucking the fluids from your body. Slow death. The Sirens lull you with their music, that sound that can only be found on the high plains.

Ask me what kept me alive all these years. I'm waiting for someone to ask me that, so I can tell them it was the music. My musical options were limited to what I had on the pad, but somehow they never got old. Music was the closest thing to a drug I had easy access to. Every night for probably a thousand nights I start my day either with Cat Stevens' *The Wind* on repeat through my solar earbuds, analog synth-crush medleys of Bach, or if I was feeling especially anxious I'd just put my ear to the proverbial window and let the sounds of the world play out like the musique concrete that it was, and then filter in some classical grindcore sounds to help ease me down.

A lot of time these sessions ended with me screaming at the top of my lungs just to let out the bile, expel the psychic phlegm that was holding me down and just breathe again. In the Corps we called it psychodramatic self-exorcism, and sure as shit you always felt better afterwards. The psych jobs told us to listen to music as a form of trauma therapy. Music and the human voice are my most valuable medicines. I'd be dead by now without the music.

And the words.

Speaking of music, if I ever crossed a railroad track, I gently put my ear to it for a long spell, just listened for anyone out there. Only ever silence, like the kind you get putting your ear to the conch shell and hearing the ocean. Industrial silence that invokes oceans. Never walked the tracks. Never. Burrowing drone mines are laced throughout these deserts, and anywhere a road crossed a railroad track was a big X that marked a spot for heavy U.S. drops.

Sometimes I'd cross tracks where an explosion had occurred long ago and shuddered at the thought of the unlucky persons who had been vaporized there. If a burrowing drone hit the pavement, they tried to drill down but always left the mark and could be neutralized fairly easily, which is to say the roads and highways remain the lifeline for anyone with a ten speed and a penchant for traveling long distances.

When the virus struck, there was nowhere to go. Most of the world died quietly in their beds. If anyone died in a public space, it was a rare thing to see from the streets. Sometimes I think of the millions of pets who died not as a result of the virus but being locked up with their owners. It's an unpleasant thought to think those animals' last meals were their masters. Any cats or dogs that got let outside surely died from licking their fur. The toxic dust laced with heavy metals made it impossible for cats and dogs to make it on their own. These are the kinds of things I think about alone down here in the vault. Wouldn't it be nice to have a cat around in a world like this? Sometimes I miss cats worse than people.

On the route out here I passed small towns through the desert, heading east from Los Angeles and taking Interstate 40 across the Mojave, jumping on Interstate 15 towards Nevada and the cratered remains of what passed for Las Vegas before heading east again on 15. I had fantasized that somehow Vegas had remained unscathed by all that had happened in the world, and I'd see the glow of the city in the distance before arriving at the strip, join their compound of isolated survivors in the desert lights. I fantasized that they might still have access to the satellites, the feed, and I could plug in, leave this world behind. When I got there, Vegas was only rubble in the dark, visible through the night vision monocular I wore around my neck.

I came east by way of L.A. because I wanted to see the city one last time. Maybe I thought I might find someone there this time, and I've got it in my head I need to keep exploring. Los Angeles is where I would have gone if I were alive, which is exactly what I did. I also think it's a human impulse to head towards home in a crisis. Maybe it's the reason dying soldiers call to their mothers, back to the source. The womb that made you. The last safe space you ever knew.

I grew up in L.A. in the 60's. In my teens my dad got offered a job as a high school language arts teacher in Grizzly Flats and we left. My mom did urban refuge architecture work and was ready to leave L.A. by the time we moved out. By California standards we were the working poor, a solid notch above the unhoused or the holdouts living in the husks of their carcassed minivans and pickup truck beds. By global standards we were rich beyond measure. When we moved away I missed L.A. and the urban shitshow that it was. Grizzly Flats was basically a suburb of Sacramento. There were trees. Depending on which way the wind blew, the air was breathable without a mask. It was fine.

After leaving L.A., which was just as empty and dead as the

last time I passed through, I got as far as a place called Kanab, Utah, before bedding down for the winter where I'm currently holed up in a very nice subterranean pad, cool enough to sleep in the midday and warm enough at night not to freeze to death. There's a functional solar air filtration system down here with enough replacement filters to last a hundred years, so I don't have to wear a respirator all the time. The dust was murderous long before the virus came.

Someone had some coin to make this place out here in bumfuck nowhere land. There're some hills on the north side of the old town, a place I can go to get a view of the world out there. I climb up there once a week and search the horizon for what, I don't know. I've started some smudge fires up there just to let anyone in eyeshot know I'm here, but that came to nothing. Reduced to smoke signals says a lot about my prospects of finding others.

FAR AS I CAN TELL from some of the fragments that remain, Kanab was some kind of western Hollywood town where they filmed a lot of those old-world cowboy shows. When I walked along the main road, there were bronze stars embedded in the sidewalk with a bunch of cowpoke names like Buck, and Rich, and Pete, and a guy named Tom Mix must have been someone special back in the day. There was a statue of him in the center of the old town square, where the birds had nested and covered the whole place in their white-speckled crap.

The birds were my initial lifeline through all this and seeing them in different oases in the desert somehow helped me keep it together, don't ask me why. The human world had been mortally wounded with collapse and when the virus struck I had every reason to believe the migratory patterns of these birds were not just continuing as ever before, but their populations were growing as the planet returned to full bloom. I have the feeling this started to happen very quickly, before I had the sense to notice it.

Was it weird to focus my mind on the birds instead of the unimaginable reality that all of humanity had perished in a few short months? Fuck you, it helped keep my mind from imploding in on itself. And so long as I kept moving the permanence of the reality I'm living in is tempered by the forward motion of my own body. The birds were a sign of that. Keep moving. There is a future out there, waiting to be found. I believe that or I wouldn't be writing any of this down.

In some kind of reverse evolutionary process, I imagined these birds devolving back into the dinosaurs they came from and overtaking the planet again. The birds were continuing without us and without human interventions it seemed like anything was possible for rewilding the planet. The birds were my first writing subject, mainly as a way to keep lists of what I was seeing, organize my thoughts and keep track of time in a way, but it hadn't occurred to me until very recently to go deeper with the writing. I regret the fact I left those early bird journals back in Grizzly Flats. The birds were the first voices to keep me company.

Kanab died long before the war, became more or less a stop in the desert judging from the endless string of motels along the main road, maybe one of the places in the early days of the simstims where city men would come out, plug their genitals into the feed, and play out their sexual fantasies with the virtual pop stars, neo-cowboy characters, and the most popular homoerotic wrestlers-in-the-round players of the day. Of course, the characters would perform based on user desires, but the wrestlers and cowboys were most popular with the closeted androsexual megachurch-militia folk living out in the sticks who would have been outcast by their communities if their true selves were openly known. If only they could have come to L.A., or Oakland, or Portland, they would have quickly realized how pedestrian their desires really were. If they ever passed through Vegas, their heads would have imploded from the sex spectacle that the city evolved into.

It's like a lot of the country was living in competing centuries, altered time zones from past and future. Sticking your genitals into the feed was practically done in public in places like L.A. and Vegas until even that became commodified, and people paid to watch other people plug into the simstims. Was it weird? Weird is a relative term. Compared to the daily bus hijackings, seasonal heat deaths in the thousands, fires that took more and more housing units each year, the aftermath of the war, collapse of global trade, and never-ending food shortages, a little public sexual exhibition seemed like a welcome release. These desert folk living in a 20th century fantasy were weird.

In general it wasn't always that these roadside travelers out here were hiding from their wives and lovers so much as the early stigma simstims had, before machine sex shifted the genderscape and overtook the mainstream. If you asked most folks from the older generations what they were most ambivalent about it was the fact that simstim sex encounters weren't with real-life people. If I had to guess, the first sentient machine intelligences were probably virtual sex workers.

It wasn't just that these encounters were with fictional, completely machine-bred characters with a multitude of choices for every orientation and fantasy, it was that the user could swap out their own genitals for the other sex, take on both or go completely android-genitalless, or even take on whatever body-horror fantasies they wanted to experiment with. Simstims made prostitution obsolete but that was just the beginning of the sexual revolution, and as an unintended consequence maybe the end of autonomous human societies.

The simstims promised sexual liberation even as the swarm algorithms were being manipulated and used as a means to create adversarial machine intelligences that learned everything they could about us. The data harvesting extracted out of the simstims was enormous because there were so many users giving up so much about themselves, their desires, their spending habits, their true identities. The sex might have been innocuous, but the machine intelligences were at work in insidious ways that go well beyond my general understanding. What I'm getting at is we were getting fucked in more ways than one.

There was a whole underground thing in towns like this, all the way into Mexico, where the simstims were also playing out various atrocity porn fantasies that were violent, psychically dangerous, and outright illegal. There wasn't any real regulation on this stuff, especially out in these nowhere towns, sort of the wild wild west 2.0. If there was a small contingent of sick fucks seeking out their criminal sexual behaviors in the simstims, the only harm they were committing was arguably to themselves. The proprietors of these places must have found the work lucrative enough to continue doing it. The world was already literally on fire, so it wasn't exactly anyone's priority to track these deviants down.

These roadside parlors were the start of all this backdoor machine sex business, sexual perversions of violence and horror so shocking even Las Vegas and its satellite cities steered clear. By the looks of this town, it could have been abandoned long before the rise of the simstim parlors, interesting now as a curio of the early days of the feed, nothing more. But the real tell that this place was a ghost town before the virus hit is the lack of mass graves.

The populated towns are easy to spot by the number of burn piles throughout town, usually covered with rocks and other debris once the pit was filled. Kanab just has an old-fashioned cemetery out past a couple storage unit sheds on the edge of town. Farther east there was an airplane graveyard, one of the desert sites where all the planes and even some spacecraft were permanently parked. I've gone out there a few times just to see the mass spectacle. Far as the eye can see, Boeings, Embraers, Northrop-Lockheeds, and their later generations from the early days of privatized space travel.

Climbing into the cockpits of some of these behemoths I got a real sense of the wonder of what it must have been like to leave the stratosphere. There's a strange almost meditative pleasure in biking past all these giant metal husks perfectly preserved in the deserts out here. I wonder if you can see them from space. I've yet to reach the other end of this place. I always stopped when I got to the large metal shipping containers buried a few miles in.

My plan is to continue east on Highway 89 in the next few weeks, soon as the weather shifts, the summer monsoons come, and this stockpile of canned hams I've been living off runs low enough to motivate me to shove off. I like the little shelter I found here, for all sorts of reasons. Someone cared for this place and then never got the chance to use it. Probably they died in the motel out front. I presume they owned the place. Never bothered to check. No reason to. I'm not superstitious, don't believe in ghosts or anything, but just the same I have no desire to interfere with the dead.

I think it's a genetic thing more than anything to steer clear of death and all its trappings. I don't like coming across dead bodies, thinking about how they died, having to look at their physical decomposition and imagine what their lives were like before the virus came and drove in the final nail. I don't need to give my subconscious more fodder for dark dreams.

A lot of the dead wrote their names, D.O.B.s, and medical histories on their foreheads and forearms, which was a practice that started once it became clear that late-stage dementia was among the earliest of symptoms. Finding these dead tattooed with their own hand-written epitaphs is just weird and to be avoided at all costs. I don't want to know their names or their blood types or the year they were born. How is that going to be useful or productive for me? All my explorations were about finding living people, not keeping an index of the dead. The Earth itself had become the graveyard of the species. Got it. What else do I need to know and what's going to help me survive?

It was an encounter with a dead man on the road about forty klicks west of here that led me to this underground cache, and prior to reading his letters and notebooks it had not occurred to me to write down a kind of post-virus life story. The dead man is the reason you're reading any of this. Not just the idea even, but his pens and paper.

I have to say, writing seems the ideal medium for communing with the dead, or maybe I should say the dead communing with the living. In all Dead Man's scribbling, he never left a name. He was a survivor, the only other survivor I've encountered, which changes my entire outlook on things. Others survived and I'm not alone. Given enough time I will find them. On the whole, this particular corpse was great news, served the mission to find survivors.

Dead Man, or maybe it was the owners of the motel, left a lot of old-world books here in the vault which sent me down a rabbit hole through the winter. I'm currently on the last book of a twenty-six-volume set of hardbound encyclopedias, which also tells me it might be time for me to move on. Winters are tricky times to be traversing the desert, because the sun can still kill you by day, but you run the risk of exposure out in the elements at night. The desert is murderously hot or cold come winter. Summertime you have the nights to cover long distances, which is what I've accustomed myself to.

I should preface that a lot of what I know about this world comes from the complete edition of a 1979 *World Book Encyclopedia*, among the first collection of printed books I've ever read. This is a bigger deal than it sounds. If you're reading this in some distant future, I realize this might take some explaining.

These encyclopedias seem like a curiously dated use of literacy to explain the entirety of the universe and everything in it. There's something comforting about thinking the whole of human knowledge could fit in twenty-six densely packed volumes. If there's a fiction embedded in these books, it's that it could all fit in there, but the entries and their illustrations are endlessly fun to read.

The rest of what I know comes mostly from my grandmother. Stories. True stories. The kinds that passed wisdom. My grandmother helped raise us, saw more in this world than her fair share. She never gave up hope on humanity. It's my grandmother that put that idea in my head, even if I don't believe it. Hope in humanity is a past-tense type of situation. Everything else I think I know carries a glaring asterisk next to it.

You can trust the words in an old-world book insofar as they cannot be altered to fit the whims of the feed or the machine intelligence that revised our perceptions of history and social reality to such a degree that when we all needed to communicate, really communicate, things were too far gone.

And it's not like all the books were burned or banned, some

dystopian nightmare. When I think about it knowing what I know now, it was something much worse. Books themselves as a technology were outdated, not the words inside them. No big mystery there. Everything got subsumed into the feed, which was great. Rich and poor alike had equal access. Everything was available to everyone who wanted it, all you had to do was access the feed. It was the technological evolution of things.

Beginning with my parents' generation everything they learned and read and watched came through the feed. Bound books stopped being printed based on shifting technologies, consumer habits, market demands, whatever you want to call it. It never crossed my mind to consider the implications of this. Why would it? No one seemed to consider the potential consequences of the feed and what that would mean for a sense of enduring thought. Strap the visors on, ride the wave, and the advertisements helped subsidize one's living expenses. In exchange you saw worlds, real ones and imagined.

The boundary between entertainment and news (or fiction and reality might be a better way to say it) evaporated. Humanity embedded itself in the feed for good. There wasn't much space to be contemplating these changes. The feed did the contemplating for you. It was sensorial overload and I'm not even talking about the simstims, which were sensorial overload to the max, the literal merger of our bodies with machine intelligence.

Every text on the feed was a living text, to the point where nothing could be trusted to be authentic. Images even more malleable. Strap your genitals into the feed and go full simstim. A lot of people went in and never came out. It was just another addiction that could eventually kill you in a long line of addictions. After global collapse, mass unemployment, toxic dust, a list of other life-threatening realities, the feed became a kind of escape back into the civilized world. Nostalgia for the masses.

Not going to lie I had plenty of simstim sex. It was fun. Never thought much of it. It wasn't that the simstims were any more or less addicting than the drugs on the street, but the simstim was basically free. And you got paid a little something for consuming the advertisements. The first person to get me thinking about all this was a desiccated corpse on the side of the road on Highway 59 out in middle-of-nowhere Utah, more than a few years after humanity went all but extinct. Very weird situation if you ask me, even in the context of apocalypse. But before I explain Dead Man, before the virus, before collapse, the foundation for this whole story has to account for the feed. Let me start there.

ORALITY, LITERACY, ELECTRACY, AND THE FEED

The feed is part of a historical trajectory that began with language. Words are the root of all this. If I had to try and distill the entire lineage into a basic history of human communication, it would go something like this, and this is important for understanding collapse, and Dead Man's rants, or I wouldn't bother trying to explain this stuff. I'm sure there'd have been someone better to try and make sense of this, but they're dead and here I am writing a history of humanity just in case there's someone left to read it. Here goes.

Orality. The first software system built on Earth. People grunted and the grunts formed words. We talked, told stories, passed them down. I feel like music belongs here too. Songs came out of our bodies. Other instruments came later. Did you ever get angry and just fucking yell, bare your teeth like some wild animal, rage at the world? If yes, that's the first language our species spoke. The language of aggression. Universal as fuck.

Literacy. We scratched the words on rocks, tablets, and later inked them on parchment. They're scratched in boulders and cave walls all over these deserts. All you have to do is look. Later, machines, old-fashioned mechanical ones, mass produced the words. This is just my opinion, but mechanical reproduction of words was a great advancement in human technologies, right next to plumbing. If we had to do it all over again, this might have been the place to stop. Seems to me before the feed literacy was the main form of entertainment other than fucking, which probably explains why so many of these books were so damn long. *Moby Dick* would have been a lot shorter if it were written in this century.

Electracy. What the old timers called movies or tee vee, or the world wide web. Did they not realize how sinister that sounded, that we might be ensnared in the web, paralyzed and then devoured? But it connected human societies in ways previously unknown. Made print obsolete. Oh, and radio, almost forgot radio.

I think of those Moon landings and everything after. One small step for man. . . . Radio was like orality gone electric.

I wonder if those Moon colonists are still up there, looking down and wondering what happened to the planet. Their only food source after a certain point would have to be each other, which gives me some solace. Millions of laborers down here working on the Moon colony supply chains. Thousands more Middle Eastern and African refugees offered jobs and a life on the Moon, the main prerequisite being that you didn't speak English. There was insidious shit going on there, enslaving these people who had already survived the worst atrocities only to find themselves entrenched deep within the Moon, mining ice or whatever rare minerals for those bastards. Space is for Everyone slogans slapped on the giant factories that ran the lengths of entire cities, shipping up actual Earth grown organic food to the Moon while everyone else ate dried protein bricks. Fuck the Noel Rodgers of this world. But I digress.

Then we got the feed. The old-world web morphed into the Global Constellation Project, or what was colloquially known as the feed. Nobody called it the Global Constellation Project. The world wide web had gone full immersion, splattered with advertisements based on your economic data set, user patterns, sexual orientations, and increasingly authored and overseen by machine intelligence. M.I.s so powerful that they could create fictions in not just words, but images, and pass them off as reality. Images that would cater to your interests, help you decide on what to purchase, how to dress, how to act, who to fuck, how to interact with other people. Social life, commerce, finance, entertainment, industry, government, the feed permeated every aspect of daily life and kept civilization running. After collapse, the feed kept the illusion that the industrialized world was still functioning, that everything was just fine. The so-called zombie-economies and their pseudocurrencies.

As the real world was descending into deeper and deeper ruin, the feed was increasingly becoming a place of escape. One of the fears people talked about was that with industrial food supply chains permanently halted, humans were interacting more and more with the wild, seeking out food by killing all kinds of animals. This was a dominant theory for the eventual outbreak of a virus like what happened, but there's no proof of that being the case. There's no proof of anything I can point to outside of the twenty-six volume encyclopedia sitting across from me, and that doesn't cover anything after 1979. The feed made the destabilization of truth possible. Dead Man explains all this better than I can, so I'll leave it to him.

The weirdest thing about the feed, looking back at least, was that human-machine sex had become the dominant form of sexual encounter and simulated procreation. Simstim sex worlds went wild in the feed and after collapse provided a real sense of personal freedom. People got paid to make virtual babies. Women had more control over their bodies in the feed than they did out in the physical world. All of this led to more feed time, more advertisements, and propped up the remnant economy before collapse just triggered the true end of the industrialized world's charade that everything was going to go on forever.

The sexual aspects were a cultural revolution happening alongside economic collapse on a global scale. Sex and death were really connected in the most intimate of ways. Looking back, I probably should have had a lot more simstim sex than I did. That ship has sailed. Into oblivion.

If you want a real mind fuck, consider that machine intelligence authored stories just like the one I'm telling now, almost certainly, since they created an infinite number of narratives with multiple variants authored for the refined idiolects and desires of the end user. By the end most of the power being produced on Earth was being siphoned off to the feed.

M.I. was the ultimate totalitarian force. It pawned off some of the threads in the feed as historical reality, others as conspiracy theories, and sometimes actual real-life events as conspiracy to discredit the veracity of the claims. Truth shrank down to the view directly out your window. The dark ages.

Everything humans ever created was embedded in the feed, and it could be altered without noticing what got altered, which is my whole point about the value of paperbound books where the ideas became fixed. Let me repeat this for you: Everything humans ever created was embedded in the feed, and it could be altered without noticing what got altered. The moment that happened should be the moment we mark the end of human consciousness as we knew it. The future of ideas was no longer a strictly human affair. And this is Dead Man speaking more than me now, but the virus isn't what killed us. The feed did us in.

Of course, humans had been doing all this manipulating for a long time, but at least it was human. Machines did it better, initially at the command of human operators. M.I. was a tool like any other, insofar as we could have used it for a multitude of ends. All this machine intelligence came about from government attempts to destabilize their enemies, so-called terrorist-paramilitary organizations—that phrase got so overused that eventually every last-standing news agency was also labeled a terrorist organization and if they provided ground security for their journalists, instant paramilitary organization designation. If you didn't have ground security you were already dead. The machine intelligence got so powerful that they could mirror any nation or organization to make the legitimate human source indistinguishable from a fake. In the end everything that came through the feed was questionable, and most dangerous precisely when one took it to be true.

If you had asked a hundred people back when there were warm bodies to ask, what was the cause for the Californian War of Independence, you'd get a hundred different answers. A few of those answers might have been true but good luck parsing them out. And if you believed the feed, things outside North America were much, much worse. I always wondered if that was just California Republic propaganda to keep us docile.

You had just as much foreign propaganda telling the opposite, how fucked we were and how great things were on other continents. People just picked a reality and went with it, for no other reason than it was what they believed. People knew you couldn't trust the feed, yet any semblance of reality you had outside your own lived experiences was shaped through information siphoned through it. A lot of what I understood about the world came from other Marines, many of whom had lived overseas before they came to California and enlisted. My time in the Corps was a transformative experience and shaped me in ways I'm still grappling with.

Words can chain the mind.

The future is surveillancing you.

Reality is shaped by those who write it.

Blind allegiance breeds blind destruction.

Freedom is the illusion of choice.

To resist is to exist.

MY TIME IN THE CORPS

The CRAF was the most diverse fighting force ever assembled, or so said the propaganda. I mean it was true, but it was also effective propaganda that increased our ranks tenfold. These were mostly first-gen immigrants from South and Central America, the Middle East, Central Europe, Africans that escaped the Chinese colonies, all of whom came to California and did two to four years compulsory military service. Time in depended on your wealth status. If you were rich, your two years of service could have been as a medic or an engineer or a dentist, maybe an administrative job, but everyone served in some capacity. I never met a fellow Marine who talked about the good life back home, and many of them were the only survivors in their family from the genocidal wars and ethnic cleansing campaigns that happened in their homelands. Once you were a Marine you were one of us.

The U.S.-California conflict wasn't genocidal or absolute, but it was organized killing on an industrial scale. There were ethnic groups in Europe, parts of Africa that weren't under Chinese occupation, and all over the Middle East that were wiped out, probably elsewhere as well. The armed forces of the world more-or-less disbanded, unable to feed themselves. Nations on the verge of collapse.

The main defense forces a country needed to maintain itself was a collection of drone-related acronyms: ACDs, PSDs, DDSs & ADCs, DINs, SIDs, DVDLAC, DDTO (inexplicably pronounced "dito"), DOSCs, and, perhaps most important, DMA. This was part of the lexicon of being a Marine. In the order listed above: autonomous combat drones, precision strike drones, drone defense systems and anti-drone countermeasures (good luck without these), drone intelligence networks, swarm-intelligence drones, drone v. drone low-altitude combat (for avoiding radar, another acronym), drone-driven tactical ops., drone-operated supply chains (which eventually became a civilian staple), and drone-managed airspace, which really came to define the true borders of a country.

PSDs (precision strike drones) were a kind of a legal euphemism that protected aggressors from being held responsible for collateral damage, another euphemism for inflicting heavy death tolls on civilian populations. PSDs were protected under international law for targeted attacks against military targets. In the end, everything and everyone was a military target, so there wasn't much need for precision.

Before I got busted back to private, I split my time between DIN and DOSC units maintaining drone intelligence networks and various logistical supply chains to the front. War in the CRAF involved highly trained soldiers operating software systems that made California, California the epicenter of the world, ground zero for drone technology advancements and lunar colonization, rivaled only by China and their satellite states.

Regarding my demotion, there's not much to tell there. I got into an altercation with a commanding officer because he was a complete fucking asshole. End of story. They sent me to Colorado to work in a prison camp for the last eight months of my final tour before being honorably discharged. In the end, it was a stroke of luck. The command center I was stationed out of ended up not surviving a series of coordinated ground and swarm drone attacks a few months after I left. I lost a lot of friends there and the anger inside me reached a high point after that.

The wars were operated and executed primarily from the corporate bunkers deep in the capital cities, sending ACD, PSD, and SID drone strikes to obliterate anything and everything that could be perceived a threat. The last phase of armed conflict in this world was contracted out to the multinational corporations still operational, a series of last-ditch efforts to make certain that if you couldn't win the war, neither could your enemies. Drone defense systems were in effect the lifeblood of the nation-state.

Drone production and their export kept nations afloat for decades until these weapons were put to use en masse. Probably the worst euphemism I could imagine after ethnic cleansing and concentration camp was drone visit. Drone visits erased more cities from the face of the Earth, more oil refineries, more of the machineries of industrialized world than anything we could pin on M.I. That was just old-fashioned human ingenuity.

We didn't need machine intelligence to destroy ourselves, so I don't buy that it was M.I. that brought about collapse. It was such a fucked-up situation that any number of catastrophes could have not occurred and we'd still be facing serious population decline. We did this mostly to ourselves. Everyone who survived had a hand in it. Everyone. The rest were victims of the violence.

Maybe the only innocents left are the unmen indentured on Mars. I sincerely hope they are having a nice life up there. I can't look to the night sky, see the red star, and not have to fight back tears. Who would have dreamed that life on Mars would have been a better bet than sticking around a perfectly hospitable planet, even if some of its systems were failing? The air here was still breathable and all that, even if it was laced with heavy metals and things that sometimes needed filtering out.

They used to say there were a thousand ways to die on Mars, and no one to come rescue you if something failed. That was before Virus (*x*). Taking a ten-year contract on Mars may have been suicidal, but if you survived, you were free to live in the colony, work above ground for the rest of your life, even have a family if you wanted one. Looking back, anyone who took that deal and survived has to be feeling pretty lucky right now. A lot of Marines migrated to Mars after the war. I could have been one of them, but I'm here.

And now after all these wars and collapse and the virus, we're back at the beginning, somewhere between orality and literacy. Looking back, maybe that was our high point. There were gods that warned about this stuff, read all about them in the en-cy-clo-pee-dee-ah. The gods we invented in our stories were at least ours, not some machine dream. According to these gods, knowledge was a temptation to be resisted, and humanity risked great punishments for seeking it out, which makes no sense to me, kind of paradoxical, but then you look at our situation and maybe those stories were prophecy just like they claimed to be. This is my grandmother talking more than me now.

Which reminds me of a story she used to tell me at bedtime. I don't think she could have imagined how relevant it might have become to explain how collapse unfolded. I'm serious, The Boy Who Cried Wolf story is basically a prophecy about the end of humanity.

There was this boy who used to play in the woods, and he would cry wolf so that everyone would come to his rescue, waking up the village and causing much astir. He'd scream and shout, people would run to his aid with axes and pitchforks, and he would have a good laugh at the villagers' expense. He did this so often that the villagers got wise and started to ignore the little shit. Then, one day, a wolf appears. This wolf has every intention of devouring the boy, tearing him limb from limb, eating his tender flesh and crunching on his bones, shitting out the rest. My grandmother had a way with words. The boy was terrified for his life, and of course cries out, wolf, wolf, wolf, as loud as he can. Wake up there's a fucking wolf about to eat me! No one comes. The wolf looks at the boy with hungry eyes before tearing him limb from limb with his powerful jaws. He devours the boy who's still screaming as he's being torn apart. She told me this and other stories to put me to sleep, which is odd when I think of it now. The sound of her voice is what I remember most.

She'd tell other stories too, Noah and the flood, a vengeance God wiping off all life on the planet, a guy, whose name escapes me now, being swallowed by a whale, things like that. Horror stories, basically. Thinking back, the biggest lesson isn't what the stories themselves were saying, or what they were teaching, but that stories are something we always carried with us, spoken from generation to generation, thousands of years before the feed, before the industrialization of human thought, before machine intelligence destabilized our world to such a degree that we were no longer able to take care of ourselves or others. This thought would have never crossed my mind if I hadn't spent so many years alone on this planet. Solitude is the best teacher.

VIEW FROM GRIZZLY FLATS

IF PEOPLE DISBELIEVED THE FEED, it was because there was reason to distrust it. I was a disbeliever of the highest order. That makes me sound arrogant, like I was smarter, but it was true, which means sometimes I was wrong about things. Like I didn't believe the last-ditch efforts to nuke all the major cities of the world was real, the governments of the world trying to save humanity. That seemed too far-fetched, even for the state of things as they were. First it was the C.R. and then the U.S. followed suit, followed by other countries. Supposedly the Caribbean Islands or Florida was a possible patient zero situation, and there were stories that Florida was annihilated, what wasn't already underwater nuked into oblivion.

There were a million stories and that was my point. Boy who cried wolf. But at least one of the stories was true. Or now that I think of it, maybe none of the stories were true. Virus (x) was called that for a reason. The (x) was the variable that never got resolved. There wasn't time to mount a serious effort. Game over.

On the subject of bombing to stop the spread of the virus, it's just as plausible that these attacks on our own cities were really global nuclear war, and the stories were being run through the feeds to try and quell the panic. Too late for that. It was too disorganized and happened too fast to call it a world war. It was worse than that. It was more like suicide by nation state.

One thing most everyone took to be real was the virus. That was easy enough to verify once you were dead, or the people around you were starting to show some very dementia-like symptoms before drowning in their own fluids. But, of course, there were stories of entire communities back east who took Virus (x) as just another hoax, and they believed that right until they shit the bed. But can you really blame them for being skeptical?

The supposed reasoning behind the self-inflicted nuke strikes was that the cities were already gone, more of an attempt to cut off the spread of the virus. I didn't believe the nuke stories until

I saw Sacramento light up in the night sky. February 16th, 2086. I'll never forget the date. For me, I used that date as the marker of a new year until I lost track of the days. Mom was dying in the next room over. She'd say, is your father okay? I'd answer her and thirty seconds later she'd ask the same thing. My biggest fear is that I would start to forget and start to answer her each time like it was the first. How many families ended like this, losing their minds together and not even recognizing it?

The virus broke down the mind and filled the lungs with fluid. I think you drowned at about the same time that your brain went to mush. Maybe the fever did it, maybe something else. Is your father okay? This was her go-to question. She started asking about people long dead, like grandmother. And then she started hallucinating things, angels, a woman named Angela, asking about the grandchild she didn't have, how I was doing on the front, never mind that the war had been over for a decade.

They were dead before they were dead. You could see it in the eyes. My father was worse off than her at the time and the best course of action was just to bring them meals and water and leave them be. There was nothing you could do. I was waiting to start forgetting who I was next. I should have been more scared than I was.

I'll never forget my last real conversation with mom, before she started getting symptoms. Her and my dad spent a lot of time at the refugee camps in Sacramento, working part time for the urban planning division assembling these temporary shelters. They met a lot of people from all over the world there.

When the first signs of the virus were happening, my mom said there were all kinds of names floating around for what was going on. This Japanese refugee called it the Kyoto Fever and said that in Japan he was hearing stories of entire fishing villages coming down with the sickness. Some were even dying.

My mom proposed an idea that really terrified me. What if this were a novel virus with an exceptionally long incubation period, like twelve months, and the virus had a way of spreading without showing symptoms or being detected by our immune systems? It was possible, she said. Before HIV was eradicated, that virus could remain latent in a person for years. Why not another even more deadly virus? That would enable the virus to spread across the globe undetected, and once inside all of us, take out the human race.

What's significant about this conversation isn't what mom told me. It's what happened the next day, when I asked her about the Kyoto Virus. She just looked at me and asked what I was talking about. I told her she had informed me about the Japanese refugee at the camp and then she says, what Japanese guy and looks at me like I'm crazy before she goes back to washing the dishes. There was a feeling of terror in that moment. The reality of the world outside my window had crept into my mother's body. Things deteriorated very quickly from there.

My mom's breathing sounded like an engine taking in water. I was holding her hand when I felt the rumble and ran to the window. We lived a ways away up in the mountains, and I saw it. It was so real-looking I thought I was in one of those feed simulations, but it was happening right before my eyes. I remember just saying out loud to no one but myself, what is that? Strangely, there was no panic. It's almost as if it didn't compute. I mean my parents were dying, would be dead in a few days, one after the other. My mother stopped asking where my father was. Soon she'd be unable to speak. My father was no longer responsive, just breathing like a fish pulled up on the dock, gasping at air he couldn't take in. I was already living in an end-of-the-world type situation. It sounds crazy, but what was a mushroom cloud in Sacramento going to do to make my life worse? All the fear in me had already been taken. Hundreds of thousands of people were probably instantly incinerated, but that was abstract compared to my parents in the next room. Like I was a Marine. Death, to me, were the bodies in your line of sight, or the targets coming through on the feed. I'm not an abstract person to begin with. But I saw Sacramento get lit up and just had a hard time processing it. It was a different story when I rode the dirt bike to the outskirts of the city a few days later. They really did it.

By the time we realized what was happening in the world, things were just too far gone. They were probably too far gone before the virus, that seemed clear even then, to anyone who bothered to look out their own window and see the state of things. Like I said, most people were perpetrators, far from innocent. After collapse, you had to be doing something illegal or underground to be making ends meet. Before collapse, anyone could get employment in California working on the drone production lines. Your work killed people, so there was that, but like I say, no one was innocent by the end.

Of course, working in one of those factories was also putting a bullseye on your back. When the schools shuttered my father worked on the drone machines outside Sacramento. But the way the feed controlled our lives, you just couldn't know what was real and what was machine intelligence creating artificial narratives, so you just worked, survived, day to day. Did China actually kill twelve million ethnic minorities? Was Pakistan actually drone-bombed into the dark ages by India and Afghan counterrevolutionaries? Was Africa as bad off as the feeds seemed to say?

I think my skepticism helped keep me sane. Like I say, the best way to verify reality was looking out your window, and that was limited to your field of vision. If you were living in Sacramento on February 16th, 2086, the virus wasn't even the worst of your problems because you got incinerated in a nuclear strike. At the time it didn't even occur to me just how many other cities shared a similar fate, or that so many people might have already succumbed to the virus. My imagination didn't extend that far into the darkness.

The future is written in ash.

Dissent is poison; swallow it whole.

Suffering is a virtue; glorify your wounds.

The true wilderness is the mind of the unmonitored.

Despair is the cornerstone of civilization.

Progress is a warm grave.

IMPRESSIONS FROM A DESERT DREAM I HAD

It was a barren desert landscape, vistas in every direction as far as the human eye could see, silent, except for the wind across an empty plain. The vibrations against the creosote, cacti and desert flora played out like music against the desert's hardened skin, giving the impression of lifelessness. The cacti persisted, roots clawing into invisible earth. Yellowed skies, cloudless and bright, blanketed the desert with utter indifference. The mountains on the horizon broke the plain, rising from beyond the vanishing point blurring the boundaries of sky and earth.

It was hot. Very hot. The sun burned anything that couldn't survive down to its simplest form. The roads baked, broke apart and were slowly being cooked away, back to dust. The roads disappeared into nowhere, marked only by the remnants of signs or long-abandoned telephone poles tilted along its course. The riverbeds and gulches cut into the earth, sometimes breaking the road in two, redefining the paths water might take when the rains came in huge bursts. In the far distance, west towards the mountains, clouds formed, and the sound of thunder turned and broke like a wave coming to shore.

Time passed like this for many years. Ancient sands traveled long distances across the desert, invading every available space, continuing to carve the boulders and canyons they helped create. Snakes, lizards, voles, mice, and other desert life burrowed and sheltered beneath the scorched earth. Violent summer monsoons brought crushing wind and rain, and for fleeting moments, the desert bloomed. Raptors scanned the desert performing graceful maneuvers that ended in violent strikes on their prey. Remnants of the occasional barbed-wire fence or stretch of telephone poles cutting across the silent plains signaled to anyone willing to cross, a path forward. At the end of the road up in the high desert was Taos. Clean water and people. Living people.

Anyway, that's how I remembered it. I wrote it down just after waking up from the desert dream. I was just floating over the desert, no fear in me of being blown up by a burrowing mine.

I woke up as the sun was setting and a heavy wind was picking up outside. I could hear the double doors rattling in the wind and wondered as I was lying in bed if that's what woke me from the dream. Or was this a nightmare? Sometimes the rattling of the door triggered memories of the large shipping containers during the war.

Most of my dreams had people in them, people I knew, experiences from the war, or my family, the things my mind was connected to. This dream was different because it was beginning to reflect the world I was living in. Normally I liked my dreams, even if they were nightmares, because they were populated by other people. This one was different, something more omniscient and non-human. I'm not sure how I feel about it. The desert was peaceful. That's enough for me.

THE BODY OF A MAN, DESICCATED

I CAME ACROSS HIM SOMEWHERE ON HIGHWAY 59 along the Arizona-Utah border. If he had wandered off the road and died ten meters off in either direction, I would have passed him in the night without even knowing. As it was, I could have practically stumbled right over his body. I might have thought the mass to have been a jumble of rags had my headlamp not caught his dried-out face staring up into the glowing night sky.

This was the closest thing to another living person I'd seen since my parents died in Grizzly Flats. I let out an audible moan, not quite a cry, but a definite sound of sorrow entering and leaving the body in the same moment. My stomach dropped and my knees loosened. The Moon was out in full bloom. I swear I looked at the Moon like I was looking for a face to explain things to me and the light up in the sky was the closest thing to a source of explanation I was going to find.

If I had to guess, no more than a year had this man been dead, maybe less. This was the body of a survivor, not of someone who died long ago from the virus. Besides the minimal decomposition of his body, people died from the virus in their homes, in their beds, not like this in the middle of the desert. The dead man no longer had the stench of a corpse, and his face looked like it had been gnawed on by an animal that found him distasteful. It looked to me like he'd been cooked out in the sun for a long time.

This wasn't a Virus (x) induced death. This guy was walking and talking all the way up until he keeled over and died on Highway 59. The emotions I felt when I found the man, gently kicked him even to feel that he was real, it's hard to describe. I was shocked, inexplicably scared, and elated all at the same time. I laughed. Here this guy had survived and ends up dead out on the road to nowhere. Why? What happened? Was he sick? You could die from prolonged exposure to this air. Did he have a respirator somewhere? Did it get blown off sometime in the past few months? Entirely plausible. Life expectancy was shorter than it had been anytime over the last century. Surviving the virus was no guarantee of immortality. Far from it.

Probably I was laughing out of nervous fear, because it had occurred to me I was doing the same thing this guy was doing right when he died: wandering the road to nowhere myself. And then I did something even more inexplicable. I spoke out loud, to call out as if anyone else was nearby.

Hello?

My voice disappeared into the darkness, absorbed by the wind. It's hard to express in words the vast emptiness of the desert, especially at night. It's almost beyond imagination to think of a world out there with no one else in it. Vacuous loneliness as far as time-space would carry your screaming voice as you yelled into the night sky like a lunatic. It's as if I half-expected this dead body to wake up and talk.

I was listening to William Basinski's *Watermusic* when I found Dead Man, which has since made that track unlistenable for me. Not that finding his body was a particularly bad memory, just that the track brings me back to that night in the desert and I don't like the feeling. Is it weird I wanted to touch him, to hug him even? I thought of giving him a burial, but that seemed like a complete waste of time. What did he have on him I could use?

I checked his pockets, and the weathered bag he'd been carrying. There was water, canned hams, plenty of those HELP slogan sheets on colorful tissue paper that no doubt he was also using to wipe his ass (I did), and notes, lots of hand-written notes, pages of them. Based on the things he was carrying it wasn't dehydration or lack of food supply that killed him. I figured his cause of death would just be a mystery forever, like the billions of other deaths before his.

Around the time I was searching the bag, panic sort of overtook me. Each morning for the last few years, before I tried to bed down for the day, I suffered massive panic attacks and sometimes found myself screaming at the top of my lungs until I about passed out. The psychic dread of feeling like you are the last human being on Earth, I'm surprised my head didn't explode from the horror. It felt like my body was getting giant, like I was growing to the size of a weather balloon or a convoy carrier, something beyond human scale. I could have these panic attacks in my head and continue whatever I was doing at the same time. The attacks paralyzed my psyche, not my body.

As I flipped through the contents of the bag, I was asking myself, why all the notes? Who was going to read them? And then I really lost it. Almost like Dead Man was talking to me, I said to myself or rather it was as if he said to me:

You are going to read them. I wrote them for you.

I was going to read them. He wrote them for me. There was a story about this my grandmother used to tell. A prophet in the desert, he either was blind, or goes blind, don't remember. He meets Jesus on the road. Always on the road. There's a transformation of vision at the heart of the story. Was this a real-life come-to-Jesus moment I was having? As if the universe had conspired to kill everyone on the planet and put me in contact with this dead guy on Highway 59? You might say no, I might say no, but here it was. It happened. That's what actually happened so this wasn't paranoia. This was real.

As I would soon learn, this man had scribbled his life's experiences in these notes, and the others I would find back at his shelter some distance back towards that cowboy simstim border ghost town among many scattered across the desert, connected by a network of cracked-up highways. That was Kanab alright. Cowboytown. Simstim, U.S.A. This man had died not far from his shelter. It made no sense.

The deserts, grasslands, and forests of Earth were consuming the remnants of our world, and you could already see that happening with the small patches of desert flora knifing its way through the blacktop. In time, the desert would swallow up all of this, of that I had no doubt. This dead man at my feet would eventually disintegrate into the desert, dry up like an orange peel before leaving no record whatever that he had walked the Earth, except maybe a belt buckle or the rubber soles of his boots. But this man survived Virus (x). I was not alone, and this was proof that others could have survived, almost certainly did survive!

Why that invoked panic in me defies logic, but that's what happened. There are so many things that have happened in my life that never got explained in any kind of sensible way. Why should this encounter be any different? The panic attack subsided. I could breathe again. The air was cool that night and it burned my lungs. I must have been breathing hard from the screaming, the panic attacks, because I remember the burning in my lungs from the cold air.

I couldn't have known it at the time, but the encounter with this desiccated corpse would end up cultivating my own disciplined approach towards writing. It's the seed for the collection of thoughts you're reading now. In my simple logic, there was reason to believe that if the dead man's experiences could be passed to me in his writing, then I could expect the same one day, for someone to find my lifeless corpse and read my life story. That actually sounded good to me, not morbid at all. Maybe I could even find a future better than this situation. Maybe a community was out there waiting for me.

But this, right here, was human communication, even if from the dead to the living. It was human communication that my body and my mind needed more than anything. Do you have any idea how difficult it is to be truly alone in this world? I had been speaking to other people in my dreams, but more recently, even my dreams started to reflect my reality of being alone.

The first thing of his I read was a piece of paper folded in his buttoned-up breast pocket. More of his writings were found in his notebooks, tucked neatly in his tattered gray-green backpack. And before I get to all his writings let me just say that despite my initial involuntary panic, finding someone who had survived the virus and lived to reflect on his experiences afterwards had a very positive effect on my mental state. His words were the only words I'd encountered since the virus other than my own.

If anyone else ever reads this, I hope you can get some sense of just how mind-altering it was to find another human being's reflections on all this. We cannot survive alone. It really hit me hard that human communication is a profound need and really the mechanism for figuring things out. Intelligence is a collective thing. I knew that from my days as a kid doing mechanics with my father. He was infinitely more knowledgeable and experienced but sometimes all it took was my outside eyes to solve a problem, just an extra pair of eyes. My mind was degrading without other voices to talk back to me.

After I found the body I was searching for something useful, maybe a fuel cell, a lighter, but I was also searching for insights into this man, a map of the body in the desert, X marking the spot where my first clue about what had happened all those years ago might reveal the nature of this horror. In his coat pocket I found a Chinese Communist Party pen-knife with retractable blade on one side and a refillable ink pen on the other, also retractable. The pen was out of ink, but the knife blade was sleek and elegant, the whole thing made of ultra-light alloy and inscribed with two Mandarin words on the side. Looked like an old war trophy, the kind of thing you'd see pop up on street markets with other curios. It was well made and had a symmetry to it that legitimized the pen-knife name for these things. I'd seen them before but never held one in my hand. I slid it in my pocket. And then I found this note, folded neatly in his breast pocket which I affix here in its original form:

Kanab, Utah, Fall 2090

Hello there. Sort of. I would have liked to write you a book but that's beyond my capacity. Also, senseless. Sometimes, as a thought exercise, I scratched out tables of contents, outlining the would-be chapters, wondering what I might say to you. There's an increasingly unbalanced pleasure in fantasy, letting the speculative imagination run wild. Reality has become the black hole from which there is no escape. That was our biggest problem, don't you think? Our collective failure to imagine our way out of this world and into another.

So what if I engage in patterns of complete vanity, delusional from the start? I'm not trying to hold onto my sanity, or the fabric of this world. Also, in case you're living in an alternative fantasy of your own devising, let this serve as a reminder that books in their paper form were an anachronism long before I imagined writing one. Everyone slowly lost in the feed, consuming blindly until the last sinew of their mortal coils was sucked into nonexistence.

I've had lots of time to think about this. If you're reading this, you've probably had lots of time to yourself as well. I wonder if the dream of every writer was to imagine a future reader and speak into an alternative future. If you are reading this then we are communing across time. The dream has already been partially fulfilled. Life on Earth still has a consciousness.

Some of our last acts on Earth were essentially forms of graffiti, which regardless of the words or symbols etched onto the architectures and artifices of civilized world all said the same thing: here I am. I exist. Look at me. The large Xs on doors to mark a house or room as off limits, the word, 'survivor,' the arrows that pointed to one's dwelling next to a number indicating the survived, the lists of names, street numbers, threats to would-be intruders, "fuck off" bullet holes etched on the side of a home or building, as if to say, 'knock, knock, is anybody home?' The inscriptions on our own bodies before our minds gave out.

Virus (x) was probably named after our graffiti, don't you think? Doesn't that make the most sense? It's too creative sounding a name for a scientist to have coined it. Scientists would have given it a name meaningful only to them, and that would have also implied some sense of understanding. A bunch of numbers and codes for their own private language. Virus (x) was a colloquial thing, wasn't it? It sounds more like science fiction, which I kind of appreciated. Hadn't our lives felt like the gap between science fiction and reality collapsed, and we were living in a world that only a madman could have imagined?

The virus' name sort of signaled our complete and total ignorance. What a brutal little fucker. It seemed to kill off the people best equipped to study it before we even knew what hit us. If the virus had a consciousness, its tactics seemed like war plans. X marked the spot, sure, but it also acknowledged the unknown variable that was murdering all of us in deranged ways. It took away your mind before it killed you.

What if the virus just caused the dementia, and we lived? That would have been an even more terrifying world. I will say this from experience. In my observations there are absolutely, unequivocally worse things than death. Oh, and I don't mean being alone on this Earth. I'm grateful to be alive. I'm talking about my life before collapse. Maybe the origin story of the name can be figured out one day, along with a way to bring back all the dead. Unburn the corpses, reconstitute the flesh. Until then, Virus (x) it is. We named the thing that killed us. That's at least some kind of exercise of power, isn't it?

There is violence in naming.

Think about it.

Either way, the final acts for so many were fundamentally literary ones. Writing in all its forms is a fundamentally hopeful, affirmative act, see? It's like vampirism without the negative connotations. You read this, and maybe you pass it on, maybe you write down your story. This may seem small and insignificant, but it is not. With enough critical thinking skills and creative invention, nothing is insignificant. The dust covering everything in my life has significance. The hawks I see each day hunting these fucking rats have significance. Fuck the fucking rats.

This shithole of a town has significance.

I actually like Kanab, to be honest.

It feels like an abandoned theme park from the 20th century, only sleezier. Even though I know it's real, it still feels like an imitation of what I had always imagined these cowpoke towns to be, failing under the myths of their own making. Cowboys and Indians type situation. What do I want to say? I don't know, but it approaches something like this: writing is the last stronghold of the imagination, and therefore the most human thing I have left to do in this world. It just feels damn good to sit here and write my thoughts down, maybe the only conscious being for ten thousand miles or more in any direction. Words carry an elegance with them.

Consider this letter my will. Take everything I have. If you find me on the road, I will you all my writings, my cache of canned hams, and a really lovely book collection, thanks to some previously deceased people who were making a life in Kanab long before I got there. I'm sick. Maybe cancer from the radiation I've encountered, eating radiated rations, who knows? It's not the canned hams, don't worry. I was sick long before I got here. No one lives forever, especially not in this world.

Who was he? No name, nothing. And on the following piece of tattered paper, his proposed table of contents. Weird:

Table of Contents, for my imaginary book. At least my thoughts remain organized in some capacity, incomplete as they may be:

How Visual Art Ushered in the Collapse of Societies
Machine Dreams: The Invention of Artificial Histories
The First Crisis: When Flesh Became Secondary
Anthroposeeing: The Age of Apocalypse and Early Revolutionaries
The Dissolution of Digital Ethics: a Confession
A Brief History of Camouflage as a Means of Understanding Machine Intelligence
The Second Crisis: The Feed Evolves, Living Fictions within Fictions
The Third Crisis: We Cannot Disprove our own Fictions
The Problem with Real-Life Sexual Encounters (A Comedy of User Errors)
Homo Imaginus: What Counts as Human?
What is Real?

I didn't fault Dead Man for his perceived insanity. Sanity was a relative term and being alone in this world untethered us from a lot of things, not just notions of a sound mental state.

I took the man's backpack, pulled out the propaganda sheets of toilet paper along with his writing papers and notebooks, shoved them into my bike's saddlebags. After inspecting the canned hams, I took those too. Why not? Little did I know there was a near year's supply waiting for me in Kanab. Left the water for some reason, maybe because in the back of my mind I thought it could be poisoned. Even though I doubted that, all of these desert towns had water reserves virtually untapped. I shoved the rest of

this stuff as best I could into my saddlebags and when that didn't
work I just ended up throwing his half-empty backpack over my
shoulder and pedaling on.

My bike was covered with all kinds of satchels and long-
distance travel bags, front and rear wheels, but I didn't leave
room to collect things. Water was my main cargo. Many gallons
of it just in case. My bicycle was my home on wheels and carried
everything I needed to make it in this world. There was an art
to it, and when you dumped everything out of the saddlebags, it
was incredible just how much you could carry.

Not that it matters to you, but while I'm making an accounting
of things, after water, the small filtration kit and tire tubes, the
next most important thing was dental hygiene. Have you ever had
a root canal? I desperately wanted to avoid having to do my own
dental work. After that, clean change of clothes and as many pairs
of clean socks as days I thought I'd be pedaling. Protein bricks and
dehydrated fruit and vegetable packs made up the rest, and they
were ultra-light. Just add water. You could find those anywhere
and their shelf life was eternity. I always carried a spork, a bar of
soap, tampons, and plenty of chapstick and lotion to prevent the
lips and skin from cracking and bleeding. That's it. That's all you
really need to make it in this world.

Strapped on the back rack were two wool blankets I had since
I was a kid, and a Visqueen sheet with rivets in it that I could clip
to the bike when the kickstand was down to make a sunshade,
which I never used but could save my life in an emergency, were I
to get caught somewhere in the open during midday. The Visqueen
had a silver reflective side and it was ultra-light. I also had a couple
solar-powered lamps connected to the bike too, and one clipped
to the brim of my cowboy hat that kept the sun out of my face
on the few occasions I was traveling in sunlight. I don't count my
solar earbuds because I wore those like earrings. Same with the
respirator, which was essentially part of my face. And I wore the
monocle around my neck, tucked under my shirt.

I made it to Kanab just as the sun was creeping over the
horizon. I continued on 59 which turned into Arizona Highway
389 briefly before coming to a fork in the road at an old CRAF

outpost called Fredonia, rode up what passed for main street and cut north into Kanab. I never used a map for any of this, just followed the signs. What is the definition of getting lost in a world where there is nowhere in particular to be? The sun was my map and my compass, and a reminder of the peril that the heat of midday posed. Like I said, my bike was my home, my center, like a turtle shell I could climb into if need be.

It didn't take any kind of detective work to find Dead Man's living quarters. His place was the only structure with solar panels that weren't caked over with a decade's worth of dust. They glowed in the purple light of the rising sun. The name of the place was the Desert Inn Motel right off the main highway. You couldn't make this stuff up. I felt like I was in one of those 20th century cinema feeds, rolling into some cowboy town like the lone, nameless cowboy. How did Dead Man end up in this hellhole of all places?

I stepped down into his dwelling, tired and spent from the encounter on the road. Sitting on a small desk, perched below the horizontal double doors that allowed one to climb into the relatively comfortable little shelter, were a pile of notebooks. He had a makeshift canvas cover that protected him from the sun and allowed him to keep the doors propped open. Nice little setup. He could keep the door propped and listen to the desert wind cut across the adobe buildings. Just then I heard a crow caw in the distance and thought this might be a great place to call home for a while. I was also on my last pair of clean socks. I fell instantly to sleep on a very comfortable mattress with clean sheets.

When I woke up I found the print books he mentioned, along with the complete edition of *World Book Encyclopedia* from 1979. They were gargantuan and took up a whole shelf next to the canned hams. Kind of amazing to imagine a world where your access to its history was limited to a collection of books.

At the time, I couldn't imagine why these people who lived here would have placed something as worthless (and inedible) as books into their bug-in shelter. But to be honest, once I cracked one of them open I got the picture. What were you supposed to do with all the time? Read. There was a literal universe of history etched onto pages for 20th century people to explore. Anthropology. Aztecs (another lost society of sorts, almost prophesizing our own situation). Animals—a whole section on animals. I mean, the knowledge placed in these books brought me to tears. I saw pictures of creatures that had gone extinct only a few short decades after these books were published. I had to read them all. This was a discovery and a reason to stay.

Before the virus, I would have tossed these books into the stove for heating, but in a world disconnected from the feed, disconnected from the living, these volumes provided a window into the world beyond my immediate view. They became more than just a way to pass the time, much, much more.

After a couple days, once I got comfortable in his old space, and having feasted on more than a few of those canned hams, I read the rest of his notes. I affix his complete oeuvre here for your reading pleasure:

The idea to write my own book came from reading other people's writing. 20th and early 21st century people. I'm talking paperbound texts in the days when trees were grown in straight rows and mass produced for paper consumption. Any text that came through the feed I do not consider an essay or book any more than I consider a photograph of a person to be a person. The real world is made of objects, get it? Books are objects with words in them. Very simple.

Everything on the feeds was a representation of a thing, and most especially and precisely when it claimed to be the thing itself. The fact that I feel the need to even state this basic fact should reflect to any would-be reader just how dire our situation really was.

Consider that the entire history of scientific exploration was meant to answer this simple question: what's real? The feed was the ultimate anti-science machine. It sought to undermine any attempt towards truth, and what I'm getting at is it was most effective precisely when it claimed to present the truth, either in news threads, or documentary realism, or just actual surveillance threads presenting things happening in the world.

The true horror, and why I would want to write a book to explain it all, is that the feed slowly, perhaps even intentionally transformed itself not into a space to represent things that were real, but to simulate things that were never true or real in the first place. Simulacra!

If I had a thesis it would be that the feed killed us before the virus did. This was the beginning of our true demise—a divorce from reality, first an ideological separation, and ultimately a corporeal one. The feed consumed the history of human knowledge historically archived in books and spit out something else entirely. The virus merely killed our bodies. Our brains were already gone.

A book is not a living thing. You can read it a hundred times and the pages might wear, the ink fade, but the words never change. Sure, the interpretation of the words changes over time, but that's on you not the text! It may be stating the obvious, but I say it in the mantra of "fuck the machine:" any text found in the feed could and would be endlessly revised, its meaning altered beyond the recognition of its original content.

The digital palimpsests of our lifetimes are, to my mind, why societies collapsed. Virus (x) was incidental, get it? Climate wars? Incidental. Famine, mass starvation, a million other physical deaths, not the point. Collapse was arguably a step in the right direction, the feed mortally wounded but still functioning so long as one had solar power and access to the satellites. It was the feed that brought about the real end. Don't let anyone tell you otherwise.

A failure to communicate is the first step towards demise. Why? Because survival is predicated on all kinds of communication skills. Okay, imagine I'm a bird, I want to mate. There's a call for that. I'm an ape I want to protect my children, there's a sound for that. Whales. A whole language for those guys still making it out there. Words, maybe, but communication, absolutely. Whales are the big ones. Talking across oceans. What are they saying? I don't know but I am certain it has to do with the preservation of life.

I found the following passages in a collection of printed books, probably among the last to be printed. Someone before me, probably a family as far as the material evidence left behind seems to suggest, had stored this collection alongside their survival materials, in a bunker next to a cache of canned meat and purified water. Smart. Where they found meat is beyond me, God bless their souls.

They must have died elsewhere because their motel above is intact and all the rooms empty. I prefer to live down here in the vault as a guest. This place was designed as a survival space and it feels very cocoon like. Feels good, just good vibes down here. Down here maybe there's a thriving world above. Living in the motel or any of the other places I've bedded down just serves as a reminder of the old world.

Why did these people leave their homes? Why was I the one to stumble onto their worldly wealth, and subsist on it for years? Isn't it strange how these things happen, without reason? Back to the beginning of all this: why was I even among the living, maybe even last man on Earth? Unanswerable questions, which is not to say they should be left unspoken.

I speak of the former occupants of this place from a place of gratitude. I do not want to go into their space, step into their children's room and begin painting a picture in my mind of their life before the virus. Instead, I lived in that well-insulated hole in ground for some time and found a world beyond my imagination in the material evidence they gifted me. The two-dozen books plus the Encyclopedia collection could be called, in modest terms, a library.

As I tore out the citations of two books, intending to take them with me when I left, I recall thinking that the authors of these texts must have known they were headed towards collapse. To the person who might find me dead somewhere in the desert, I carried around these cuttings in my pocket because I wanted you to read them. Who else? Yes, you! Don't you get it, my body is the book, these scribblings an extended string of thoughts from my mind to yours. We were once a great species, goddammit! We sent people to Mars, even if it was to extract mineral wealth and destroy more lives in the process! We built vacation homes for the rich and famous on the Moon! Their lived experiences were among the highest rated threads on the feed!

Not going to lie, I slapped the receptors on and lived on the Moon for a while too. Who didn't want to walk through those greenhouse gardens of paradise, or take long walks on the Moon, climbing the craters and coming up on those amazing vistas of the Blue Marble? Everyone living on the Moon was beautiful, healthy, and had a vitality that we could experience vicariously through the feeds. We had it made up there, didn't we? Who didn't want to escape their life and live in the new-aged cinema of distractions?

Or maybe those lost Martian colonists will come back one day and save us. I have to imagine they created a society up there that will outlive ours, whatever's left of it here. I had to laugh when the Martian nationalists sent the Terran ambassador back to Earth in a body bag. Was that real or another fiction from the feed? As serious as things were, if true, those Martian revolutionaries were not without a sense of humor. If you don't get the context, the Martian revolutionaries were threatened over and over again about their fragile dwellings being like "body bags." All it took was a small projectile to pierce their outer shells and everyone inside would die horrible deaths. Sending the ambassador in a body bag was the retort. Needless to say, they started living in the lava tubes after that. Turns out it's hard to find people hiding on Mars.

I remember in my early school days, the biology lesson that life on Earth began on Mars—fragments of the Red Planet breaking off creating Phobos, Deimos, and a million more would-be moons that splintered off and became missiles across the galaxy. Some crashed into Earth, and some had microbial life on them and they evolved in our carbon-rich oceans, and eventually became us and everything else that once crawled over this once Blue Planet of ours. Who's to say the Martian colonists won't came back to Earth one day and make a new Eden out of the old ruins?

So here are those torn-out passages I've been telling you about:

"One of the defining qualities of the psychopath is an individual operating in an unreal world. What we are witnessing in the seemingly final stages of industrialized societies' dominion over the planet are large segments of national populations operating in diametrically opposed fictional realities. One could argue that primitive societies operated in much the same way, existing within a social reality that relied on spirit worlds and other *inventions of the human imagination. These ways of being providing meaning in people's lives and upheld the social fabric of communities—they are in fact part of what has always made us human.*

"We have always used stories to make sense of the world. The turning point, where collapse will manifest as the final outcome, is that industrial world pitted imaginary worlds against one another on a scale that only a global connectivity could have fostered. The result has been profound genocidal violence, paradoxically, a violence that can never be proven to have happened. Not just because the witnesses were themselves annihilated—to have witnessed the inside of a burn box was to have perished within it—but also because machine consciousness has infected all aspects of media communication beyond the point of its utility. The human conflicts are ultimately battles for the survival of ideas, ideological strangleholds on entire peoples.

"Ideology has always been the purest form of power that has ever existed, and violence its primary weapon. This time, the weapon has taken the form of the so-called 'artificial,' machine intelligence. There is nothing artificial about it. Never before in human history have our tools, weapons or otherwise, returned our gaze with an intelligible consciousness. It may be incorrect to even call it a tool—it was an agent insofar as it acted on its own. Tools don't generally think for themselves. What were the conditions of life near the midpoint of the 21st century that such a reality seemed to terrify almost no one?"

—Dr. Barry Siegel, *The Collective Psychosis*

And this clipping too:

"Machine intelligence was not the monster that we made it out to be. M.I. was manipulated into an instrument of war used by national governments and rogue terrorist organizations to destabilize their enemies. Left to its own devices, M.I. would have likely maintained an ethics that superseded human behaviors in almost every case. Life on Earth, quality of life on

Earth, would have fared much better if we had allowed M.I. to act autonomously."

—Aarya Brahmbhatt, Towards a History of Non-Human Intelligence

These decades-old books and the others I read in that subterranean bug-in shelter were proof, at least to me, that prior to collapse and the social reality that my generation lived in, there were people advancing complex ideas about the state of things and the human/M.I. dilemmas that would allow for collapse. Once the feeds took over, this kind of human-centric deep, complex thinking was essentially eradicated.

The Collective Psychosis told a history of how the roots of the unreal world and the rise of the feed had its origins in primitive societies, in the fictive stories and mythologies they told themselves that were once necessary components of a society in order to make sense of the world around them. These stories were taken as "true stories" and in a word, generally referred to as "religions" or "cosmologies."

Regardless of ideological foundations, religion was always the great organizer of human behavior, and in some sense the last fictive story created by our species before machine intelligence took over the job. Religion, by comparison, proved to be a child's thing compared to the power of M.I. to transform our realities, to have us act against our own collective best interests. The best case I can make for M.I. consciousness is that it told stories as a means of constructing its own reality. That's as human, or post-human as it gets.

Siegel spells it out more succinctly than I can: take the example of a Judeo-Christian worldview that accepts the inventions of God and Devil as real. Not as metaphors for the struggle of a human ethics, but as objectively real entities, even if we can't know or describe them.

Okay, no problem, right? The believer still accepts the world around them as being real, the powers of observation, scientific inquiry and the tools that allowed us to do things like get to Mars, or mine rare minerals from deep under the ocean. The trouble comes when the feed emerges as the dominant instrument of human communication. In a social reality where God-Devil paradigms are accepted as real, it then stands to reason that demons too are real (since they're extensions of the devil). And since the devil is fundamentally a trickster/shapeshifter character, it also stands to reason that he and his agents can take any form.

In the old world, there was no feed to alter visual representation in ways that could be believable. This stuff was limited to our imaginations, or the occasional dream or hallucination. Visions. Siegel points to early proto examples of this prior to the feed, like some instance in France where people had ingested some bacteria found in bread that induced hallucinations and then bad things happened—some proto-LSD substance that rattled their brains and blurred the boundaries of reality. Or in the days of the early American colony, there was the widespread belief in witches, which had the effect of controlling so-called unruly women and settling land disputes with one's neighbors by making various accusations of witchcraft followed by burning the family's women alive.

In actuality, the hysteria that played out in places like Salem, Mass. serve as early indicators that ostensibly civil societies could also accept a fictive world of devils, demons, witches, and other manifestations of creative mind as real. These and other examples serve as evidence that human societies were susceptible, even doomed by the advanced M.I. technologies that came to dominate the feeds, and that religion was the human-run software that allowed us to fall into the trap of fictive social realities. Suddenly the devils of our imagination became manifest. Plato's Cave Syndrome as Siegel called it.

He's clear on the point that all societies required stories as a means of survival, and in the early millennia of our species' existence, the fact that human societies took their fictive stories to be "real" had utility as a mechanism for preserving culture and societal norms.

Siegel's analysis starts to cross over into my own training as an archeopsychic extractor, which was born out of advancements in neuroscience coupled with cognitive psychology, which was fundamentally about making sense of a human beings' inside world. Simply stated, inside world is what goes on inside of our minds, and encompasses the world of emotions, self, and identity.

World religions were a dominant part of inside world throughout most of human history. The crisis had to do with internal world manifesting in external world, which the technologies that played out in the feed made possible. That's the crux of the crisis. Our visions *and manifestations born out of religious narratives could now be made manifest, but M.I. did this in much more subtle and nuanced ways than devils and witches. This was not a simstim game of the 20th century or one of its offshoots. This was complex audio-visual rendering of completely fictive worlds extending a web of endlessly verifiable connections that created a historical narrative that included the whole of human history. The Devil was real. You could see him. He spoke to you if you wished it. The feed wove the threads of your desires into a new fabric of psychic reality.*

New mythologies yield new histories. This reworking of historical reality had the effect of reshaping a global understanding of reality. If that wasn't bad enough, the competing realities that were presented to different factions across varying societies led to the wars and eventual collapse of industrial world. In the end, the "devils" and "demons" being bombed and exterminated by the millions weren't even human so how could these acts have been interpreted as anything but just and necessary? Even in old world, dehumanizing a political enemy was nothing new, the feeds were just that much more effective, the final weapon of the world's autocrats and despots.

But as with any war, the use of a weapon on an enemy also implied the possibility of being killed by that same weapon by the other side. War was always a relationship with death more than ideological concepts, a willingness not so much to kill as to be killed.

I performed extractions knowing it was a simple calculus of us or them. The feed was the last answer in the human exploration of weapons of war. The result was not just annihilation, it was a re-rendering of historical reality. We killed not only ourselves, but our pasts with it.

People are expendable.

Religion is self-incarceration.

Every system is designed to protect itself.

Beneath the skin, we share the same wounds.

Transform despair into action.

ARCHEOPSYCHIC EXTRACTION
AND OTHER CONFESSIONS

THE MORE I THOUGHT ABOUT DEAD MAN'S DEMISE, there was a strong case to be made that he just broke with reality entirely and started walking into the sun. I wondered if he was even sick. Suicide by desert seemed possible. If that could be true for him it could become true for me.

I was holding it together but my mind felt like a delicate thing. One wrong move and it would shatter. No coming back. Those kinds of thoughts entered my mind and then heavy dread would hit me in waves, the panic attacks where my body kept expanding outside my skin. I just tried to ignore it. That was impossible but fighting it would have been like fighting a tidal wave in the middle of the sea. They had to be endured.

Bicycling through the desert seemed to help. I pedaled faster and my mind would sometimes just shut off. I could breathe again. Coming back to Cowboytown each morning it created a routine, and the routine was helpful for my sanity. Bicycling the desert highways by night, reading encyclopedia entries until morning light, and sleeping through the heat of the day became my routine. The routine was a means of maintaining sanity.

Something happened here before the virus, but I could never figure out what that was. Without intending to, I had explored every building and road in Kanab and its outskirts by virtue of spending so much time here. The town had been abandoned maybe during the war, or collapse, who knows.

The history of this place was speculative at best and caked too deeply in desert dust for me to want to dig any deeper. I couldn't find the remnants of a liquor store, which in the end makes me think this place had been abandoned even longer than I'd thought.

My adopted cache of canned meat and water had probably been two-thirds exhausted, but I could supplement this with foraging in the valleys that were a half day's bike ride from here.

Foraging had previously taken up so many of my waking hours and the beauty of this cache was I had time for leisure, time to read, for my newfound writing, to stay busy but on things beyond surviving. Over the years this had become increasingly difficult.

Also, I don't think I've yet mentioned I was on my way to Taos, where I had a dream that the water up there in their aquifer was still drinkable. I think it was a dream, but it was based on the reality of Taos as a kind of beacon of the Western Republic. Taos became a kind of capital city of California's central corridor.

Even before the war, cities like Phoenix had long been abandoned. With more than half the year crossing the hundred-degree threshold, what few industries and government services still existed fell back and retreated to higher elevations. The cities that were spared from becoming ghost towns were up at the higher elevations, and Taos was one of the few cities to expand and prosper at the expense of so many others.

It was an ancient city populated by the Indigenous long before the Californians, and it had transformed itself into a metropolis over a decades-long expansion. There was also an aquifer that provided clean drinking water, so anyone who could afford their way into Taos took it. Every wealthy California, Californian had a second or third home in Taos, as a matter of course. If there were survivors out there, Taos was a city they might flock to. It's what I was doing and I had a strong hunch others would eventually make their way to Taos too. In the back of my mind, Taos was always a kind of terminus for me.

And so for the better part of a season I survived on the well-preserved pig flesh and capsule water listening to the wind and reading the entirety of the 1979 edition of *World Book Encyclopedia*. When I needed a break from that, I returned to Dead Man's collection of notes:

Archeopsychic extraction was born out of fields previously known as neuroscience and psychology. Psychology was among the earliest, most primitive forms of attempting to understand the human mind before we had the advanced scientific tools necessary to properly analyze the chemistry and fundamental organic processes inherent to the brain and its development. Our brains are without any doubt the most complex machines to have been produced on Planet Earth—more complex than any machine invented before or since, human, artificial, otherwise.

Missteps in the early study of the mind were made, profound misdirection in the understanding of human behaviors. There were extreme cases: brain mutilations in the name of pacifying patients beyond the scope of normal behavior, complete miscategorizations of sexual orientations. Brain mutilations, or surgery if you're being generous, were as old as humanity itself, trephinations having been performed as far back as the paleolithic period a few million years ago. It seems our ancestors always had a fascination with the cranium, and why not? What's going on in that skull? Only one way to find out. You have to kill a thing to study it proper.

Basic foundations of the field were later proven to be completely misleading, even false. There were crude over-emphases on phallic preoccupations, the human quest to seek out meaning, and a clear bias to what was once known as heteronormative sexual behavior, now viewed as an archaic category for the understanding of the nuanced complexities of human sexuality. But these early people simply didn't know what they didn't know. The brain was mostly a mysterious organ strapped inside our skulls, its processes indistinguishable from magic even to its end-users.

We now know human sexuality was always far more complex than the old-world binaries, yet sexual identity remained the key to understanding the "why" of the human mind, a kind of cornerstone the house was built around, and ultimately connected by. When sexual desire crossed into the machine world, when humans started connecting their sexual pleasures to machine "bodies"—artificial intelligence—a new evolutionary process was underway.

Unlike organic evolution which took millennia to complete, this technologically assisted evolution took months and years. And as even schoolchildren learn in biology classes, when environments shift too quickly for a species to adapt, extinction comes next.

There was a kind of Aristotelian justice to the whole thing. Human industrial societies had brought about the collapse of Earth systems, leading to multispecies peril on the planet, life mostly unable to adapt to the drastic changes we'd brought about. Now humanity was *facing that same crisis on two fronts—external world in the planetary ecological situation, and internal world as redefined by the feed.*

Interacting with the feed, we were both human and also becoming non-human, transforming into part of something else. A dissenting camp in the field argued the evolutionary process began earlier, when brain-M.I. interfaces were implanted in human skulls, but in the grand scheme these changes were more cosmetic than evolutionary, like wearing piercings, or jewelry on one's body. It was the act of sex, not the interface that marked the shift. Sexual intercourse is, after all, an evolutionary mechanism for replicating a species. The pleasure is more than incidental though, quite necessary for the species' survival. When our minds accepted sex with machines as a part of social reality, we were extending a kind of human ethics and morality to these machines. In a word, trust.

"Sex drive," "hard drive," and a million other turns of phrase made light of the situation, but humanity was falling into a trap. What no one bothered to ask was, beyond the pleasure and the so-called "infinity erections," what was being replicated in this process of sexual interaction? But that's not the right question. It wasn't what was being replicated—nothing was being replicated, machines can't reproduce like organisms—it was what was being reinvented. Reality itself was being transformed. Simply put, our five senses were becoming less useful as we connected our brains directly to the feed. The feed provided the sensorium, another reality.

20th and 21st century science fiction had more-or-less prophesized these kinds of things, so it was no wonder that the feeds would use these fictive stories and blend them with reality to create an endless web of conspiracies. Science fiction has always paved the way for the future. Just look to the moon as the prime example, with its endless string of stories. Science fiction became fiction, and fiction came to replace our interpretation of historical real-world. Before social reality was entirely reinvented, the old structures of thought and history had to be discredited and dismantled.

It's difficult to define what became of the human/M.I. sexual connection because those processes were still underway when collapse occurred. Virus (x) was a completely unrelated set of events that humanity was ill equipped to address on a global scale because our communication systems could no longer be trusted. Would the virus have wiped out humanity either way? Maybe. Of course, there's no way to know. Consider the threat of nuclear annihilation that has hung over our heads for 150 years. It's very probable that nuclear holocaust was avoided on more than one occasion thanks to the timely communication of world leaders, nation states, and the basic ability to trust information that your own tools and technologies were delivering to you.

Why am I even writing about this? This isn't a rhetorical question, I am asking myself this now, as I live a life alone in the world. Well, my real-time answer: I am talking about this now because I have time to think about it, and it is on my mind, but I understand the issue is purely academic at this point. Machine sex, unreliable feeds that sowed complete distrust in all forms of communication, and a virus that came to wipe us all out. It's a weird world, no two ways about it. Why am I still alive when it seems no one else survived?

I had no idea what Dead Man was talking about much of the time. But it was interesting to hear his voice in my head as I read his words. Someone else besides me. The closest thing I'd had to a conversation with anyone else in a long time. Sure, I could have read anything and had the same feeling, but this guy survived the virus. What if there was some clue in his writing as to why or how he survived? We had something in common in that we were both immune to whatever happened. If there were more of us maybe we could repopulate the Earth. I hadn't even thought about things like this. Dead Man was a profound sign of hope.

Increasingly, I felt the need to get to Taos, but what was a few weeks or a month compared to the years I'd already spent searching? Feasting on the canned hams and other freeze-dried rations I uncovered in the compartment beneath the bed, I read on:

I was trained in the field of archeopsychic cognitive development, a branch off the early neuroscience tree. My intentions as a professional practitioner were never to hurt human beings, quite the opposite—to bring peace of mind to those who most needed it. I once would have said these words: *I am a good person*. Now I can't even imagine having been that person. I can say I never meant to inflict pain, and yet through political systems that ultimately were intended to destroy all opposition, one was either a cog in that machine or destroyed by it. I willfully acted as the former.

Existence outweighed any quality of existence, and that was a path humanity had been on for some time. Many of my colleagues committed suicide. Some early on, when they saw what was being demanded of us, others later, having realized what we had done. I've come to conclude that archeopsychic extraction may well be the penultimate weapon invented in human history, presuming the Global Constellation Project to be the last.

In the simplest of terms, archeopsychic extraction enabled human minds to be read like an image feed, with the scenes presented out of sequence. But the images, the shots, the sequences, sometimes even entire memory streams or "episodes" were as coherent as watching a feed thread itself. And we could achieve all this with or without the permission of the "patient."

We would access the brain through the ocular cavities, plugging our fiberoptics directly into the medial aspects of the temporal lobe where memories were housed. This entry point was discovered as part of the practice of lobotomy. We forced the sensor ends right through the eye sockets until we penetrated brain matter. This process induced massive epileptic seizures that, despite having the patient medically restrained, in almost all instances caused spinal fractures in the patient, often causing permanent paralysis.

Once in, the extraction process separated declarative, episodic memories from the semantic ones, like general knowledge which generally had no actionable intelligence value, unless someone was a spy or counterspy and you could assess things like native tongue and thought patterns that were tied to origins and by proxy, national identity.

The declarative memories would appear in our closed-circuit feeds on thousands of virtual threads, which could be analyzed by human analysts but of course the swarm algorithms were able to parse out the potentially valuable memories that related to our intelligence efforts. Even still, this required human intervention to analyze and *interpret—a power of imagination that sometimes expedited the process over machine analysis.*

Our victims were always called "patients," up until the end when we dispensed with all trappings of humanity, and just called them "living" or "expired." They were almost always classified as unprivileged belligerents, regardless of their actual status, because that designation provided us the legal protections to provide medical care, which extraction fell under. The entire thing was a farce. These people were treated as non-humans and the so-called treatment they were receiving was classified as non-lethal even though that was completely false.

We could extract from the dead just as we could the living—the brain maintains an electrical charge for a short time after death, even as it begins to decompose. Sometimes, for legal paperwork purposes, it was easier to deal with expired subjects, which were asphyxiated immediately prior to our cables going in through their ocular cavities. I preferred the dead. Sticking cables in through a living person's eye cavities never brought a feeling of pleasure, at least for me.

As I was reading Dead Man's notebooks, any admiration I might have had for him quickly evaporated into a feeling of dread. I swore an oath to the Republic to protect it from perpetrators like Dead Man. I would have happily killed him in another time and place.

The war was over, but almost certainly he was an American enemy combatant. This guy would have tortured and killed me if our paths had crossed on the wrong side during the war. But there was an intelligence in his words that kept me curious. To be honest, it disturbed me that I was still curious. I wonder if I should have just stopped reading his entries.

California had outlawed archeopsychic extraction and all other forms of torture before the outbreak of the war. It was considered a war crime everywhere in the world except the United States, China, and their proxy governments. Even the warring Islamic nations and their warlords forbid it, citing extraction as firmly against the will of Allah. Not even the most extremist mujahadeen implemented extraction on their enemies, which should tell you everything you need to know. The dehumanization of extraction became another piece of evidence against the United

States as an inherently evil enemy. The CR didn't torture its prisoners. It didn't even take prisoners.

Incidentally, I found this in the encyclopedia, under the heading, "brain" and had to laugh, don't ask me why. But if I had to guess, I think the laughter was a defense mechanism to the sheer terror of what I was encountering in Dead Man's diatribe. He was one of the perpetrators, a war criminal if there had been any tribunal left to convict these people. The encyclopedia entry on brains read as follows:

> *The human brain begins to decompose within minutes of death, which is faster than other body tissues because it's about 80% water. The brain liquefies and eventually reaches a paste, or fluid-like consistency as proteins break down and putrefaction occurs. Rotting starts at normal temperatures after about three days, and the brain is essentially vaporized within 5-10 years.*

I read on in his notes:

After extraction, the victims almost never survived, and when they did, they would have wished themselves dead if they could have formulated a thought. Asphyxiation prior to treatment became the easier method, but it prevented reacessing the brain once decomposition set in.

I see those people in my dreams. We all did, though no one admitted it. It's almost nightly, as if there is a population of human beings that I'm able to interact with only in sleep, like their souls became part of my consciousness. This was the thing about extraction. It blurred the lines between conscious and subconscious, perceptions and memory. I still have the dreams. The sound of the cables going in through the fleshy parts of the ocular cavities stays with me, and the resistance of human brain matter to our prodding. Flesh makes a sound when you penetrate it.

Last night I had a dream about a man who was a subsistence farmer on a small plot of land in the desert, adjacent to his tiny, dilapidated dwelling. I'm not sure he even had electricity and cannot recall the reasons why we performed extraction on him. Why they

*were attempting to farm there was a different matter altogether—it
had not rained in this part of the desert in years, but his deep-drilled
well kept him and his family alive, probably a remnant from one of
the U.S.-backed incursions into Afghanistan.*

*This was during the final occupation when if in a village of one
thousand people, we believed one person to have intelligence on the
movements of our enemies, we eradicated everyone in the village to
find the one. In my dream, I return to the man's house to ask if I could
plant some seeds on his plot. I think I must have talked to his son, the
man not being home, and the son allowed me to sow the seeds. I recall
using this exact phrase, spoken in my broken Pashto and translated
into English as follows: "may I sow the seeds in your garden?" Why
I should remember that phrase is beyond me. May I sow the seeds?*

*When I returned, in the dream still, sometime later to check
on my seeds—they were beans, nitrogen fixers in an attempt to
somehow improve the soil that I knew was beyond saving, completely
contaminated, poisoned many times over (this man and his family
were already dead, in real life, not the dream)—when I returned in
the dream though, the father was home, and he did not know I planted
the seeds in his garden. He did not let me check on the seedlings and I
got the impression he was hiding something, like he had tilled the soil
where I had planted. This produced a feeling of great panic in me, as
if it were the most terrifying of nightmares, but it was only the seeds in
his plot. In the dream I somehow knew this entire family were ghosts,
but the dead controlled the living, set the rules.*

*Sometimes my dreams are like this. Other times they are of the
actual horrors committed, and as real to me as the day they occurred,
but mostly the dreams have the illusion of being non-violent human
encounters. I guess you'd call them wish fulfillments played out in
fantasy. In my dreams my Pashto is much better than in real life. I
oversaw extraction on the farmer and his entire family. None survived.
If memory serves, we gained nothing useful from them. If we had
gained intel from them, it would not have changed anything.*

*The true horror, and I must not have been alone in this, is that
machine intelligence's ability to render virtual spaces real rendered
the differences between reality and non-reality to be non-existent. Of
course, anytime anyone has a dream, we simultaneously ask ourselves*

if even the dreams are authentic. Waking life was an increasingly difficult thing to prove. Every dream is a reminder of this. After the war many of my colleagues fell into M.I. virtual spaces and never came out, their bodies left to dehydrate, starve, shut down. I tried the simstims but there was no pleasure in sex for me, in human touch, simulated or otherwise. The human body disgusted me.

There were so many other crises at that point, suffice to say many were willful participants in their own demise, so-called "peaceful suicides" perhaps thinking stepping into the M.I would provide a means of escape, which in the end, it did. This was just one more way to die, hardly the centerpiece of global crises at this point. We lost the war and our national problems were compounding so heavily at this point.

I also performed extraction on fellow archeopsychic extractors—those who were deemed traitors or counter spies. It's the closest I've come to reading my own thoughts laid bare, as if looking at the reality of life in a reflection pool. My conscience does not allow these victims to go away. The mind continues to mind against our wills. Why is it that we don't even have control over our own thoughts?

I always knew what I was doing was horrifically wrong, profoundly immoral, and yet I did not resist. The more I did it the less it bothered me. I am guilty, and my survival was predicated on being of service to the war effort.

Now, the question is not one of what I have done. It is a question of what I will do from here: how I will act from this point forward? The answer to this question lies before you. This collection of thoughts and private meditations is what I offer as my atonement, pathetic as it may be. To whom? Who knows. I do not ask for forgiveness. In any case, none could be given. The violence and destruction of the industrial world has come to full fruition. Who is left to judge us, to hold account of our crimes against our fellow man? My actions do not deserve to be absolved, but they should be remembered.

Tomorrow I'm packing out and headed west. I'm not sure how far I can go, but I want to die on the road, facing the late-day sun. I think it will be quicker that way.

Godspeed, fuckers.

Finance is a mental disease.

Sacrifice your body for transcendence.

Bodies are the civilized world's currency.

Violence nurtures the gardens of paradise.

Pity the hopeful for they are weak.

Civilization is a perversion.

OLD CHURCH AT SAN FELIPE PUEBLO

Somewhere along the road from Kanab to Taos, after I'd left the comforts of Dead Man's subterranean dwelling, I passed a small village, an Indian reservation, San Felipe Pueblo. Everything looked to be in such a state of disrepair that it was possible that the place had been abandoned long before the virus struck. Once the rivers ran dry or enough people got sick from the toxic runoff in places like this, they were given housing in one of the refuge cities in California, California. But this place looked like it never had a boom period. It was just some dwellings come up out of the mud, made of mud and eventually going to return to mud. What would be left of this place to suggest it even existed in a hundred years?

I'd taken the long way up to Taos, figuring I'd pass through Albuquerque and Santa Fe. Albuquerque was evacuated during the war, since it had major military positions and everyone knew it was going to get drone-bombed into oblivion, which it did. I was stationed there briefly before getting shipped off to eastern Colorado. The demotion that saved my life. After the war some of the town was rebuilt but evidently not enough to merit a nuclear strike during the last days of the virus. If there were survivors in Albuquerque and they had made a home there along the arterial roads, I would have found them. Santa Fe was also intact. This boded well for Taos. If Taos had been bombed out, it would have been the longest bicycle ride in history for no good reason. But what else was I going to do with my remaining days?

The Indian village was off Interstate 25. It played the same song as all the others. That low hum of the wind whistling off the edges of corrugated metal, weather-worn adobe, and burnt-out creosote patches. Sometimes in the desert wind I thought I'd get the hint of a generator running, but I knew that was impossible, not just because petrol had gone bad the better part of a decade ago, but because everyone was gone. It was just that simple. If someone were alive, it would not have been in an inhospitable place like this. It would have been hard to survive here before collapse.

Curiosity kept me exploring these places, knowing I'd never be coming through here again in my lifetime. I stopped for a moment and brushed the dust off my forehead, the only part of my flesh exposed to the desert. I dusted off my cowboy hat on my pants leg with a few swings against my thigh and put it back on my head. I didn't venture off the main road, but I couldn't find the familiar pile of rocks and rubble that came to mark the mass grave burn pits necessary during the final phase of the virus, when folks were on their own and the conventional wisdom was to burn the bodies and bury the remains in whatever you had laying around.

Bound by law was the language of the times. Bound by law to burn the bodies. Hard to forget a thing like that. Bound by law to burn your parents, your brothers, sisters. Your child. Bound by law. Thinking back, as horrific as that was, there was still the belief that the rest of us would make it. We didn't.

I passed a church, a small white building constructed of horizontal clapboards. It seemed out of place in a village comprised mostly of adobe walls and corrugated metal. Where was a church not out of place though? This was the architecture of colonization after all. A church in the desert is the stuff of surrealist paintings but here it was. It was an ancient structure and strangely beautiful against the purple-red-orange hues and the dust-caked structures that surrounded it. The sun was barely making itself visible over the low mountain ranges to the east, always my favorite time among my waking hours.

The desert was a whole other creature when the sun was at full tilt, and solar noon was a murderous place to be without shelter. I had at least a few more hours on the road before bedding down for the afternoon sun. I didn't want to stay here if I didn't have to. Maybe I'd make it to Santa Fe was my thinking. The way this world was, there was Lunar World, and Solar World. Lunar World was a hospitable planet, welcoming even with its cool breezes and moonlight mesas. Stars out and the Milky Way above. Solar World sucked the water from your flesh and tried to murder you by noon.

Out front of the church there was a sign, and enough letters were still hanging on that I could make out the phrase:

No weapon formed shall prosper.

When I read that, two thoughts came to mind, the first immediately and the second sometime later after I had left the village. First, I constructed a whole new imaginary history for the village. Maybe these people had retreated here after the feed went down, or better yet, maybe they were religious holdouts who saw the feed as the defiler of spiritual sanctity. I mean, they weren't wrong. The zealots were living in a reality of their own devising thousands of years in the making, but in the grand scheme of things, the Christian sects that broke off from the feeds must have been better off than the rest of us, at least for a time.

Supposedly back in Utah there were a bunch of these folks who colonized the place centuries earlier. Brigham Young I think his name was. Talked to God, took many wives, standard cult protocol. Young had an encyclopedia entry. Wouldn't it have been grand if I had come across this church and found a bunch of survivors living out their lives as if it were the 19th century out here? I'd take it, praise Jesus. We were living in the exact end-of-days world these religious zealots prophesized about. Where was the return of the Messiah and how would anyone find him? These old-world stories were so quaint, as if the whole of humanity was in walking distance of each other.

But in reality these reservations were basically prisons, spatial and technological outcasts from industrial world. If anyone had a chance to make it out alive, it would have been in a place like this, or at least that's what I told myself just to maintain the possibility of finding someone else. Otherwise, what was the point of trekking halfway across the continent? Dead Man was proof enough that I was not alone on the planet and so I continued onward, towards those mountains. There was always a voice in my head telling me stories to keep me alive, to stay positive, to forget the bad things and forge ahead.

I didn't even stop bicycling, or try the doors of the church, which were barricaded shut with a thick set of rusted chains. To give my fantasies that kind of legitimacy seemed like a slippery slope. The path to insanity. There wasn't anyone here, or anywhere for that matter. I didn't see any graffiti on the main road. If anything, that was proof that this place wasn't just abandoned long ago, but that the road itself wasn't even an arterial east-west passage. If it weren't for the rising sun, I wouldn't have known I was going in the right direction.

Taos was that way. The way I was going. No weapon formed shall prosper. That is the ultimate, final truth, isn't it? Ancient wisdom to explain what seemed increasingly to be the final explanation for future's end. This was possibly the last answer we were going to get in the aftermath of an unlikely doomsday. The wind was still playing its song when I left the village in the dust.

As I was leaving, I thought places like this gave a lot of credence to the idea that the virus had a dormancy period of many months or years. Otherwise, how did people in places this remote also succumb to the virus?

It was somewhere along the road as the sun was rising that the second thought about the crumbling church sign came to me. I can't believe in all these years I hadn't thought of this. Stupid. What if Virus (x) was a weapon? This was an unprovable theory like all the rest, but entirely plausible, wasn't it? And unlike nuclear holocaust, life on Earth would persist without humanity, maybe regain its footing. Maybe the death cults had fulfilled their wishes.

There were terrorist groups and even a couple leftover nation states with their cult leaders that advocated various human extinction movements, some voluntarily by simply ceasing to procreate, others through violent means. Spaceflamers, Patriot-Front Exterminists, The Afro-Christian-Jihadist Alliance, The Iowa Rewilding Project (The IRP did actually end up wiping out a large swath of the Iowan population by simultaneously poisoning various water sources), the New-Age Earth Liberation Front, and of course the Human Extinction Liberation Project, HELP for short.

HELP was very active among the farmworker unions that survived collapse. HELP was like the Pepsi-Coke of cult death squads, very popular and found everywhere. I loved reading their slogans, pasted throughout the urban centers of the small towns

I passed through, where they advocated for all kinds of strange things through their enigmatic phrases.

In my earliest days after the virus when I was crisscrossing California, if I saw one of their sheets of slogans—3 to 6 lines of dueling meditations on bright tissue paper—I'd shove it in my rucksack. It was doubly efficient insofar as it was both reading material and toilet paper. Finding toilet paper was harder than I thought. It required going into someone's home and having to subject myself to that or finding a mass drone logistics center which was always in the middle of the desert somewhere. The few times I'd tried that I ended up spending half a night searching in the darkness for the supplies I needed and then the rest of the night figuring out how to transport it back on the bike. It just wasn't worth the effort. As buildings started to decay, the smell caused a kind of depression in me. I preferred to stay outdoors. Light and nimble was the way.

HELP had a practice of flying surplus government drones over the desert and dropping hundreds of thousands of these thin tissue-paper sheets over anything resembling a town or a road. This had been going on for decades, since before the war, and had continued up until the end. There were still artists and old-guard Gen-Phoenix tree hugger types doing weird shit post-collapse, maybe more than ever. *Art is a weapon* kind of mantras.

We are the architects of oblivion. Galacticide is the final solution. Embrace ruin. Tyranny weeds out the fragile spirits. Our ashes fertilize the future. Man invented genocide. The pamphlets are hard to miss in the desert, colored in seven-mile orange, neon lime green, drone yellow, and other fluorescents.

Finding the occasional hot pink or neon-lemon yellow paper caught on the spines of a cholla cactus in the desert was like finding an Easter egg in the middle of nowhere, or like cracking open a fortune cookie with strange scribblings written in succession. In a world without stories they were better than nothing.

I collected them and it wasn't just for the toilet paper. I enjoyed them, wondering about the intention behind each line, reconsidering each truism in the context of life without humans, seeing which of these prophecies had come true. The colorful papers also made great placeholders for my chapter markers if I ever wanted to go back, which I never did.

It was weird, but collecting things in these single-serving ways, making lists, keeping track of the birds I'd seen, these kinds of random acts helped keep my sanity. My collection of HELP slogans goes with me wherever I go. I enjoyed reading them and even tried to avoid wiping my ass with some of my favorites.

Who knows, maybe one of these groups had pulled off the unthinkable and ended the species once and for all. But this kind of thinking got me nowhere, running in circles. Just keep pedaling, moving forward. No weapon formed shall prosper. Maybe there'd be answers in Taos and if not, all the same. Keep on riding while you can. No weapon formed shall prosper. I thought if I stopped and got to thinking about things from the past too long, I'd end up just like Dead Man. I'd come to the desert to quiet my mind and on the whole I'd say it was working.

Up ahead off the interstate I could see a long-abandoned electric charging station decaying in the desert. It was on a perpendicular two-lane highway that disappeared into the mountains. No telephone or power poles to follow. Those kinds of roads were dangerous. The road out here could quickly turn into a sand-covered path and without the posts to guide your way it seemed all too easy to find yourself continuing straight, and when the road took a turn, finding yourself stepping on a burrowing mine and having your legs blown off. I told myself this was not the way I was going to die and avoided these roads at all costs. Besides, it stood to reason anyone else alive in this world would make it to the main roads if they made it at all.

As I approached the station I wondered how come these ruins were always such aesthetically pleasing experiences. Were they beautiful because they were crumbling in the desert, and secretly we wished the end to this industrialized disaster on a planetary scale? No weapon formed shall prosper. The phrase was stuck in my head like a Cat Stevens tune, but the Bible slogan was unwelcome now. Words seemed to carry extra weight in this silent world.

I was sure I'd find some shade inside to bed down for the long day ahead. I was thirsty and needed a break from Cat Stevens on endless loop. I saw a roadrunner cross my path and wondered what it was doing all alone out here. They must be light enough not to trigger this sea of land mines. No one is that lucky. The sun was coming up and even with a steady breeze to give the illusion of coolness, I could tell by the way it was looking at me it had murder on its brain.

Unseen forces shape visible realities.

To be human is to be in perpetual denial.

Reality bends towards the grave.

YOU ARE THE ONE WHO DID THIS TO ME

HOW IS THE VIRUS SPREAD?

We don't know.

Is this a vector-borne disease and how do we stop its spread?

Vector borne is a possibility. We don't know. On the one hand, mosquito populations, for example, have risen dramatically over the past decade in equatorial parts of the planet, and on the other hand, we're also seeing widespread collapse of pollinators. Is there a correlation between these changes and the appearance of this virus? We don't know.

What is the death toll, or do you have a general idea of death toll?

I can't speculate right now. We, I, am doing the best that I can in attempting to serve the people of California.

Who is currently in charge of the country? There are rumors the president has succumbed to the virus. Your predecessors have all succumbed to the virus. Are you afraid for your life?

We are all afraid for our lives. Fear is what's helping keep us focused right now. As for the president, I presume the president is still able-bodied and leading the nation. They spoke with me earlier today via feed. I can confirm at this time the vice president and her family have expired.

The government is doing nothing to stop this. You are responsible for protecting the people. Telling us to burn the bodies of the dead or face extermination is not governance. This is a fucking joke! Fascists!

I am doing everything I can to protect the people. My responsibility is to the living.

Doctor, you have provided no answers!

Okay, okay. Please. Let's try to remain . . . I'm doing . . . I'm doing what I can.

Please forgive my colleague. You just stated you don't know how the virus is spread, but have any advancements been made in understanding how this virus is being transmitted? What efforts are currently underway to make some headway on this?

I am unaware of any advancements being made. We don't know how it spreads. It could be a parasite, something else, we just don't know. The medical personnel who have attempted to treat those with the virus were among the first wave of its victims. The individuals most qualified to answer these questions are no longer with us. It appears the transmission rate for medical personnel has been very near one hundred percent. Hospitals are not being staffed because there are not the critical numbers of doctors, nurses, and medical care providers necessary for treating those exhibiting symptoms. Right now we are not primarily concerned with resolving how the virus is spread. We are locking down the country, and with the cooperation of the United States, Mexico, and Canada, locking down North American borders.

Who else is serving in the Ministry of Health, doctor? Who else is assisting you with the crisis?

You are speaking with the entirety of the Ministry of Health.

Late in the day, I wake from this one sweating. It's the tail end of that same nightmare, streaming endlessly on the feed that is my subconscious brain. This doctor from the Ministry of Health was the last human voice I heard speaking to me in this world, and she's stuck there in an endless loop.

It's hotter than usual, so hot my face stings a little from the heat. The vents in the roof must be locked shut. My eyes open and I see a man standing in the corner of the charging station waiting room. I was sleeping on the floor in the far corner opposite the large glass windows. I laid there motionless for at least ten minutes, maybe more to see if the man would make a move. He was partially obscured by the long shadows that were coming in from the poles outside. This place had been converted from a petrol station half a century ago and the shelves were barren. It was a skeleton of its former self.

The man doesn't move. He's not a trick of light. Did he follow me here or had I trespassed onto his space? He comes into focus as my eyes adjust to the light. I remain still, not wanting him to know I'm watching him. No weapon formed shall prosper? Fuck that, I'm a goddamn Marine. I am a walking talking weapon and very hard to kill. At some point I come to enough to realize this is crazy. I whisper, still sleepy, hoping this can end peacefully.

Who are you?

No response. He stands there motionless. I think he blinks. His eyes go dark and light up again. This time I speak more forcefully, still a croaked whisper:

Who are you?

I am the one who did this to you.

Oh, fuck. Is this real? I can't remember if I said that out loud or just thought it.

He just stands there, silent. I wait. No response.

Are you real?

Again, nothing. Everything felt real, my body in a sweat. At this point I thought I might be dreaming and told myself to wake up. I'd had nightmares like this before. Seeing people in my dreams doing strange, violent things, was nothing new to me. Those dreams felt good to be with other people, back in the land of the living. It was the waking up that terrified me, being thrust back into a world where I was completely alone.

I'd even had dreams where I woke up in the dream only to see my dead parents rise out of their literal death beds, zombies. They'd just stare at me, motionless. Those nightmares caused great terror in me when they were happening. I'd had dreams where masses of black corpses, charred and smoking were rising up and coming at me, their limbs cracking off as they lunged towards me. I'd had dreams I was locked up in a metal shipping container being burned alive, screaming for these motherfuckers to stop. I'd wake up from these nightmares as if someone was standing over me, shaking me violently to wake me up but of course no one was ever there. Those dreams didn't scare me like this one. This was different. This wasn't a dream because I wasn't sleeping.

I am the one who did this to you.

I thought about a weapon and felt stupid for not preparing myself for some kind of violent encounter. Why would anyone want to hurt someone in a world such as this? But I'm a Marine. Jane Ballard. Survived. Being lethal was ingrained in me, but here

I was at the mercy of a strange man in the middle of the desert on a continent devoid of other people. I remembered the knife in my rucksack.

I am the one who did this to you.

None of this was real, of course it couldn't be. I thought for a moment this could be Dead Man. For one, he didn't look like the dead man, or my rendering of Dead Man in my imagination. His face was much fleshier and softer than the skin-wrapped skull I came upon in the desert or the embodiment I had created for him. This could have been anyone.

Seeing and hearing things was nothing new. Every noise, every creak, any sound whatever I wanted to attribute to someone else out there. Seeing another living person would have helped make the dread subside. I wanted to see people, so seeing the specter of the dead man didn't seem that strange to me. But how long had he been standing over me while I was sleeping? That's what terrified me. How long had it been there?

I still thought I might be dreaming and continued with a measure of uncertainty. Some time passed. Neither of us moved. The light outside was almost unreal, that orange-red hue that comes in the desert before the sun disappears for good. There were clouds this time and they were lit up in a grand spectacle that you have to see to believe. One thing I always thought the feed could never do as well as real life was clouds, the light at sunset, and the grand spectacle of the desert in that late-day light. The sunrays glittered in his eyes, and they would go dark when he blinked. He blinked slowly, like his eyelids moved in slow motion. I thought he might have come a step closer but wasn't sure. Regaining my courage, thinking it was time to fight or die, I broke the silence:

What do you want?

Same thing as you.

Okay. And what is that? I want you to disappear. Get the fuck out of here.

I can't. You know that.

No, I don't know that.

Yeah, you do. Your mind is inside my body. I am a projection from inside your head. That means you can't get rid of me. We're in this world together. You took my soul on the road in the desert, remember? Go back to sleep. Everything is fine. I'll wake you when it gets dark and we can move on from here.

I asked him, as if logic could get me out of this: if you're inside my head, then you know what the church sign said back on the reservation.

He stepped out of the shadows. In that moment I felt the adrenaline that came before a fight, and then he said it: *No weapon formed shall prosper.*

This felt more out of my control than ever before. I was losing it. I had a moment where I said to myself pull it together and I did. My breathing was short but I pulled out and tried to breathe deep. I heard it speak once more, in a whisper. I can't be sure but I thought it said:

I'm a good person.

When I looked up, Dead Man was gone. A long time passed before I had the courage to move. There was a profound feeling of loneliness in me that I have not felt before or since. I don't know why that is. I just stared out into the desert, through those large glass windows and tried to imagine that the world was still out there like it was before the virus. The apparition was gone and I was alone again, listening to the wind as I fell back asleep.

Half asleep, half awake, I thought of a story my grandmother recounted about Jesus in the desert, the devil appears, offers all kinds of things. That wasn't going to help me here. Dead Man didn't seem to be offering me anything at all. When I woke up again it was night.

Oppression is forgetting.

To embrace despair is to surrender.

We cultivate extinction while celebrating growth.

Progress demands sacrifice of the weak.

Fear is the currency of power.

DRONE BOMBING ON THE CALIFORNIAN FRONTIER

THE ROAD FROM KANAB TO TAOS looked very much the same as it had near the end of the war. Sand, heat, and the skeletal remains of the U.S. drones that never reached their targets. Prior to carpeting the deserts with burrowing mines, the United States drone-bombed every last town, village, and man-made structure in advance of a ground strike that never came. U.S. infantrymen were decimated in a host of DDTO (drone-driven tactical ops.) strikes in rear-operating bases like St. Louis, Lincoln, Sioux Falls, and Houston, and their main forward-operating forces cut off in Colorado, where they were also wiped out by more DDTOs followed by ground forces coming in to clean up the mess.

The tentative forward-operating bases essentially became islands in a sea of CRAF Marines and DDTO strikes attacking from every direction. In the States' bravado to drive from the Mississippi to the Pacific, towards the seat of government in Sacramento, they spread their drone defense systems too thin and were eventually annihilated. The survival rate for U.S. infantrymen that penetrated that deep into the Western Republic was zero, unless they defected and just blended in with the locals, which was possible. The U.S. government was warned that American troops invading the California Republic would not be taken prisoner.

The U.S. claimed we were violating international law to which we were signatories and were in part the originators of those laws. What the U.S. failed to recognize was that we were a new nation and had signed no such treaty. It's beside the point that Europe was in a state of ruin and those treaties weren't worth the paper they were written on. The deal the U.S. got was get the fuck out of the C.R, or risk death as unprivileged belligerents, which is what they called us. American citizens, soldiers or otherwise, had no legal standing in the California Republic, ever.

The lack of legal status was intended to prevent U.S. attacks but all it did was get all those unlucky Americans conscripted into battle killed. The Americans had a joke that California had solved the housing crisis and the homeless problem. All it took was the mass murder of millions of the poor and unhoused. The reality is that the Americans became the butt of that joke, sending in their poor and dispossessed to be slaughtered in the war.

The drones were another story. Once the States realized they would not be able to take territory in the southwest, or anywhere else, and as retaliation for what the CRAF did to their armed forces, they delivered hundreds of thousands of low-altitude combat drones armed with burrowing land mines. These LAC drones dropped their payloads in an endless stream as far west as Nevada and Eastern Oregon. They were hard to stop because they avoided radar and even if you got half of them, each one of those little fuckers carried upwards of 400 burrowing mines. The attack lasted for months, through the winter of the last year, when there was no hope for U.S. victory. For every LAC drone the CRAF destroyed, ten or fifteen got through our defenses.

You have to realize the United States had spent two decades stockpiling drones, not just for border defense and various failed incursions, but to keep their economy from completely crashing. This worked both ways, as the CRAF had plenty of drone strikes to mete out from the west coast, resulting in most of the American Midwest becoming an inhospitable desert that could not be traversed, even by road, if you could find one. The largest land mine field in the world currently exists between the Eastern Front and the Mississippi River. By landmass, it's almost a third of the former United States of America.

And the territories farther east were already succumbing to endless droughts and increasingly powerful wildfires that made any attempts at crop or cattle-raising an exercise in futility. It was truly biblical stuff. At one point locusts actually did destroy the final attempts at crops in the lower Midwest. The climate shifting and violent storms that happened with increasing regularity made industrial agriculture all but impossible. The soil was practically sterile by this point anyway and required massive fertilization to produce anything edible.

The New American Dust Bowl extended farther and wider than anything one could have imagined, and food production was a true national crisis. The southern tip of Florida had produced massive food stocks for a century, but that region of the country was succumbing to rising king tides and hurricanes that swallowed coastal cities and flooded interior farmland. The south in general suffered massive floods and mudslides from the hurricanes that kept getting stronger and creeping deeper and deeper into the Appalachians. Food production was a thing of the past in Florida and much of the south. For all these reasons and more, the U.S. desperately tried to hold onto its western territories, but it ended in more violence and destruction than if they had just allowed the western states to secede.

In my initial crossing of the desert, once I got out of Nevada and moving closer to the front, from almost any given point I could see the wreckage of a fallen drone somewhere in my line of sight. The deserts were littered with these metal husks, struck down in their initial attacks. In the last days of the U.S. drone strikes, a lot of the landmine drones doubled as Kamikazes destined for California, and laced with nuclear warheads that could level a city upon impact. Across the desert, you could see the occasional disruption in the flatness of the landscape where one of these nuclear drones had been taken down, cratering the desert with their giant payloads.

For reasons beyond my understanding, certain cities were deemed sanctuary sites for civilians, and both sides agreed not to strike so long as military aid or movements were not made within 100 kilometers of these cities. Taos and Denver were designated refugee encampment cities and throughout the war, not a single shot was fired in these cities. Amidst the hellish fighting that was going on across the American west and Midwest, if you could make it to one of those cities you were safe.

Denver was designated as the city for any westerner who didn't want to secede from the U.S. to travel to, and they were promised safe passage back east. They had to give up their land holdings and pay an eighty percent tax on their net worth to leave, but the Californian Republic made the deal to allow dissenters to pack up and head east. We called these traitors *gusanos*, but were glad to see them go, as the west was overpopulated as it was. It was almost exclusively white folks who took the deal, old money for whom an eighty percent cut of their generational wealth still left them millionaires. Good luck back in Cleveland or Buffalo or wherever the hell you ended up. I'm sure more would have gone back too, were it not for the rumors that the *gusanos* were being rounded up and mass executed.

Salvation lies in destruction.

The void is godless, pure, and free.

Genocide is a symptom of industrial society.

Use violence to destroy systems of oppression.

Worship beneath the altar of ruin.

EDGE OF TAOS

I followed US 64 until I came to Rio Grande Gorge Bridge, arriving sometime in the early morning hours. I was dealing with some early morning sun, probably already ninety degrees but dry, almost no humidity. The dry heat was dangerous because you couldn't feel it killing you, sucking the water from your body until you're a desiccated corpse in the desert pedaling into oblivion with a rucksack full of notes, senseless and lost in this world. Too late to die now. Gone too far. Drinking lots of water was the solution to this problem. I was too close to stop and I could see signs of the city glittering on the horizon across the gorge.

It was a spectacle to be seen, the famous bridge to nowhere. With the wind picking up and the sheer height of the bridge over the river below, I dismounted and started walking across. Both sides of the bridge were wrapped in large cylindrical spirals of razor wire that rose about three meters above the railing. At about every fifteen meters there were signs in English, Spanish, and Mandarin discouraging individuals with suicidal thoughts from jumping, as if the razor wire didn't already make that clear. The wire could have been climbed, but only for the most committed.

I passed the sun-faded leafless plastic stems of a makeshift memorial. The denuded plastic flowers were wrapped with metal wire around one of the rusted vertical posts of the bridge. A few plastic petals remained on the stems, but everything was faded to an almost translucent white. The plastic might last forever, outlive the bridge even, which was destined to collapse like all human constructions. I presumed someone had jumped from this point, and these plastic flowers were what remained of the memorial. I swear to Christ I felt a sadness there for no rational reason. Why should this single deceased person from some distant past make me feel anything? It occurred to me I might have felt something for the mourners too, who had also faced death, with no one left to memorialize them. Bodies in a burn pit. Maybe I was feeling sorry for myself in that moment. Some kind of self-pity for being the last woman standing. Looking down at the river about a hundred and fifty meters below, I shuddered at the thought of being crushed on the rocks.

I took out one of my water bags and sucked it dry. Thirstier than I thought. Before me was the Taos plateau. A murderous place by virtue of its very qualities: heat, extreme heat, toxic dust, no shelter, not even a stick to burn at night, and the instruments of punishment splayed out on a vast landscape that turns your body into a leathery husk if you wait long enough. Not going to lie. It was a sublime spectacle.

Was there something wrong with me that I found this place so strangely attractive, comforting even? The colors, the sound of the wind, the jagged edges and deep wounds cut into the Earth, as if giant gods had warred here before time itself. This shit was objectively beautiful and worth the long trek across California. This was probably the best I'd felt since the virus and all that happened after. Movement across this desert and time in it was bringing me some measure of peace. If I found survivors in Taos, it would bring an end to my life of global alienation. If there were no survivors in Taos, so be it. The desert was as fine a place as any to be alone.

Acceptance was a process that led me here, to the desert, to the ancient bridge over this gorge cut into the Earth over millennia. The morning light across the mesa and the path the gorge forged into the vanishing point created a kind of visual poetry that drew the eye in, deeper and deeper until you were in it. Here I was, crossing the deserts, eating the dust. Somehow the edge of Taos was even more beautiful than the rest. Maybe I was hallucinating.

Don't get me wrong, the desert terrified me, and crossing it was like holding one's breath underwater. There was a hard limit to what you could sustain. Traveling at night in absolute darkness except for the beam of the solar lamp marking the way, I followed the giant metal power poles that stood like skeletons glowing under the moonlight, and continued until the sun told me it was time to bed down for the day.

It occurred to me I had been strangely content eating my canned hams, reading the encyclopedia entries, and listening to the wind back in Kanab. I could have stayed there even longer. All these thoughts came to me on the bridge over the gorge which was more than just a literal crossing into Taos. My life before I crossed the bridge and after was marked by this moment and I seemed to have a premonition of the moment's significance before anything had happened.

On the bridge, something came over me and I stopped at the halfway point to take in the view down below. The Little Rio Grande was a long ways down, diminutive looking from way up here, but there was really nothing tiny about the gash in the Earth that I was looking down into. I'd never seen the Grand Canyon except in the feed but this felt like something similar, to be observed with great reverence.

The cliffs on both sides of the river birthed the occasional tree struggling for light, climbing skyward as its exposed roots held on for dear life. It was a sight to see in the morning sun. I think the reason I had to come to the desert was that it was possible to be out here before the virus and be alone. In that fantasy I could pretend the world was just as it was and my parents were back in Grizzly Flats and billions of people around the planet were going about their business while I was out here in the vast loneliness of the High Plains desert.

Coming into the small towns brought that wave of reality that could best be described as depression. I'm not going to lie, sometimes I would ride my bike through these nowhere ghost towns and just scream at the top of my lungs the whole way through. These weren't moments of madness so much as trauma therapy that helped release the pain. I always felt better after a good yell, my voice gone but who needed that anyway with no one to talk to? As I was having these thoughts on the bridge, considering if now was going to be one of those times when I started screaming out loud, I saw him.

Dead Man stood in my periphery, about fifty meters out on the eastern bank of the gorge. I thought I might have been dehydrated, seeing things, I mean I definitely was dehydrated but either way he was standing on the far edge of the bridge, blocking my path towards Taos. Time to go. I got back on my bike and peddled past him. He just stood there and watched me go. No response, nothing, but I swear I heard him say something as I was just out of earshot. When I turned back to see if he was still there, the bridge was empty and the black western sky was hinting purple-blue as the sun rose in my face, lighting up the clouds in an explosion of red and oranges bleeding into the black.

This is going to sound crazy but I think he was realizing I wouldn't be seeing him as much if I found survivors in Taos. He was a bitch-ass jealous ghost, envious of the living. I actually felt sorry for him. I had let him in and now he wanted more. I told you it was dangerous to interfere with the dead. Should have left his body unmolested, left his notes to rot away with his remains, let someone else get possessed by this dead guy. When I turned back towards Taos that's when I saw what I really should have seen from a hundred meters out but was so transfixed on the gorge and the grand vista surrounding me. On the large rusting metal sign, spraypainted in fluorescent orange letters were two words that nearly stopped me in my tracks. *Taos Safe.*

The body is a vessel for destruction.

Delight in the devastation of existence.

Violence is love's purest form; surrender to it.

Your silence is tyranny's strongest weapon.

PART 2

AT SEA

It's been years since I've written anything personal down. Not a word except for my bird journal which doesn't count. I keep that in a separate folder, more like a list of birds I saw starting in the first days of the plague years. As far as the real writing, I feel like it was in large part a self-medicating response to loneliness. Dead Man's gift to me.

Life in Taos completely transformed my place in the world and how I felt about it. Rebirth. Year zero. New world. My words go to the others. Why spend any time alone talking to myself in these notebooks when I have them? The years in Taos transformed me. When I found the others, Dead Man's invasive thoughts subsided. I was myself again, whoever that was.

For the first time since I watched my parents die in Grizzly Flats, Sacramento go up in the nuclear strike, there was something inside me besides the aching dread of loneliness. I found others. They found me. We gave each other purpose and joy and a semblance of hope. A lifeline out of the deep hole that I know they were feeling just like I was. Living like each of us did before Taos was punishment that none of us deserved and yet somehow, we endured, found our way together.

Through them a process of letting go of the dead, the people each of us loved and cared for in our lives, a process where we could move on and tether our futures to each other has been happening. Family isn't the right word for it. A clan. Maybe, a tribe. Yeah, a tribe. We are a people and we are bound to one another. But after a time I think we all needed more. We needed to find others, claw something more than just five of us alone in this world.

I will say I think I liked them better when we weren't all holed up on this ship together. We're on a nuclear-powered mining vessel, the *MCV Nerrivik*, headed to South America on the prospect of finding others. Rogue radio transmission gave us a destination: Cabo San Pablo. I'll explain everything in time. I just think the writing works better when I follow my stream of consciousness. I can't force this into a linear story. That's not the way memory works.

What I can say for sure is Tobi, Maria, Priya, Danh and I are the last people I know to be alive in North America. It's a big continent. Almost certainly others are out there. The math was always on our side, even if the cities we'd encountered seemed to suggest otherwise. Together we make up the last remnants of the Californian Republic and the United States. Those old ideas don't seem to have a place in this new world anymore, do they?

If there is to be a new world with humans populating it in any great measure, it will be a world without borders, flags, armies, masters and slaves. We're like a tribe of hunter-gatherers, or post-virus anarchists maybe, not out of some radicalized politics, just old-fashioned survival and a search for coexistence. Balance might be the word for it. We serve each other and in so doing serve ourselves. Isn't that the definition of community?

There is honor in this. What is civilization, anyway? What were the words that propped it up, and the actions civilized people took to maintain their way of existence? Was there honor in it? Was it good? Was there quality, true quality, as in the things we created were good and beautiful and worthy of being replicated?

There was simulated reality, and drone production to fight the last wars that would ever be fought, organized by non-human machine intelligences to maximize destruction and death on our enemies. And we had sex with machines more than each other. It was a dehumanizing world and I'm glad it's gone. Does that make me a bad person?

Here are the words I would use to describe the five of us: fidelity to each other, honoring each other's experiences, beauty in strength and resilience, respect for life. Joy. Love. You're alive so I appreciate your animated body in the world. Say and do what you will, we accept you as a living, conscious being, and so therefore are one of us. Sometimes we didn't agree on things. We loved each other's bodies when it was convenient for us, and there was pleasure in the human touch.

These people walked through the fire. I walked through the fire. What can I say about what's happened? Virus (x)? The extermination of the human race? All these words I've written, all my thoughts, many more never committed to any kind of page, not a one of these things can do a damn thing to explain what has happened to this world. And so what? Why should I or anyone else have the answers?

Humans couldn't be content with the inside world, finding some semblance of peace within. The bile inside us became manifest in the external world. I saw the ruins of these things all around me. Drones, millions of them, and burrowing mines across an entire continent. You can't even walk the desert except on a road without fear of being blown up. My bare feet almost never touched the earth. This world is the manifestation of our poverty of thought, our impoverished imaginations. Our seeds were literally burrowing mines that sprouted on impact with human footsteps. We dreamed of death and destruction and so is it any wonder we mass-produced it? Have you ever seen a living breathing person vaporized in an instant, their energy transformed into nothingness? We could have imagined alternative realities, but we didn't.

I'm looking out my porthole now. Watching the sea breathing out there, covered in fog. The sunrise has made a strange glow of things out there. I'm nightshift, like I prefer it. When I wake up maybe this fog will have broken, and I'll be able to see the horizon.

I was the last of five to arrive in Taos. Here's who I found:

Tobi's from Virginia. Or West Virginia. Does it matter? It does, and I'll ask him and get it right later. Tobi rode his bicycle all the way from Virginia to Roswell making him by far the person to have traveled the farthest, and the only American in the bunch.

The rest of us were Californians. Danh from Chicago by way of escaping Vietnam. Maria came from Texas and Priya from eastern Colorado, some small town, Fort-something-or-other. She says she's from eastern Colorado like that's supposed to mean something, distinguishing her corner of the State from the other quadrants of Colorado so as not to confuse the four of us as to where she's from. During the war Coloradans held the line on the

Eastern Front and there's some pride there, which seems foolish in a world like this. I haven't told them I was in the Corps. Everyone has their secrets, and their reasons for this. Why not me?

I still scream into the void, though not as often as I used to. I told the others that this was just something I did to quiet my mind, shut shit down. And you know what? They didn't think I was crazy. They joined. A week ago Priya found me inside the little orange lifeboat on the bridge deck screaming my lungs out. The lifeboat looked like an oversized orange sarcophagus with tiny circular windows and was a great place to hide and block out the endless drone of the ship. She knew what I was up to so she climbed in, closed the hatch and screamed with me.

Sometimes back in Taos we'd just yell and cry and rage and go berserk and then the walls are down and we're free. From the pain comes something else and we're laughing, looking into each other's eyes and it feels good. Somehow the horror of our pasts is washed away and we're laughing at wordless jokes.

Until you've stood in the deserts on the edge of Taos, half-naked, freezing, out of breath at high altitude from running from invisible adversaries, your voice cracked and bleeding from the screaming, you don't know what it's like. The sickness inside us can be released through the voice, through the screams, through the expelling of the psychic demons we carry. The body is a conduit for all sorts of things.

Look out at the ocean, teeming with life, creatures eating each other in an endless orgy of consumption. But it's natural death, not machine death. There is no weapons-grade M.I. software running this system, no swarm drone arsenals coming to annihilate us for no good reason. It's life and death in a system that reproduces itself endlessly. No need for human interventions. I can't explain it, but the distinction is everything. It's beautiful and terrifying. What if the (x) in Virus (x) stood for human? Doesn't that resolve the equation, bring equilibrium back to the planet? What if the virus wasn't a problem but a solution?

As I write this, the ship is swaying, somewhat gently, and the rain jackets on the wall look like an invisible hand is moving them back and forth. That invisible hand's name is gravity. It rains out here in the Atlantic. I can't think of the last time I saw rain. The air is thick and heavy. It's been about a week at sea and I'm still getting used to the perpetual motion. The first day out of port in Massachusetts it was sunny and blue. At about midday a fog descended over us and has not lifted since. Are we even moving? I feel like I'm on another planet out here. An ocean planet.

There's still fresh fruit on this ship. Before we left port, after the long trek across the continent, we hacked every banana hand we could from the wild stands that were growing in the forests along the coast. The humidity on the east coast was brutal. Mosquitoes big enough to carry you away. My skin reacts violently to the bites, swelling up to the size of a ten-dollar coin. We're not in Taos anymore.

I saw two whales today. I got a good look at the first one, two points off the port bow. The other breached dead ahead about twenty yards away. I should note Tobi insisted we learn the nautical terminology. The next thing I saw was a large circle in the ocean on the starboard bow where the whale had decided to go down deep. I hadn't even noticed I was crying, feeling something so joyous and peaceful that I would just be writing a bunch of platitudes if I tried to describe it. You had to be there. There is life in this ocean so great and so free that it goes beyond anything we could ever relate to.

Today the ocean was rolling, maybe four-foot swells. It's like the ocean is breathing. As I look out my stateroom porthole, there is a thick fog out there still, visibility about fifty yards, and the light is just coming up. Glowing gray light diffused and so thick it looks like you could sleep on it. With the fog I can't tell if the ship is moving or the current is rushing past us. To be honest, my sense of time and spatial relations has definitely been compromised on this ship. Time to get some sleep and forget about all this.

Today we passed the Florida coast and the remnants of the old Space ports. The original NASA site is mostly underwater, submerged in an inland marsh of sorts. This prompted Tobi to tell me one of his conspiracy theories. I mean he doesn't call them conspiracy theories but Tobi is the reason stories like The Boy Who Cried Wolf exist in the first place.

Tobi said that when NASA cleared the marshlands and dammed the waters so they couldn't drain at low tide, the mosquito populations were eradicated, which was the point. The mosquitos also happened to be the main food source of the Dusky Seaside Sparrow, supposedly a bird that was facing extinction due to the diminished habitats along the coast. This was well over a century ago and the bird was relegated to this last piece of Florida swampland, hanging on for dear life. The bird ended up going extinct, the last known survivor expiring in captivity in Central Florida somewhere. He says the last bird was owned by Disneycorp but sometimes his stories are so outlandish I just nod and go along.

He said scientists ended up calling it the Dusky Seaside Sparrow Paradox, because to explore space, and eventually other planets, it meant driving Earth into further ruin. Whether or not the story about the sparrow is true, the underlying point holds. I will say it was eerie seeing the remnants of the spaceport ravaged by hurricanes and basically slowly sinking into the sea. It looked haunted through my monocular, like you might sight the ghost of Wernher von Braun walking the halls talking about rockets to Mars.

Tobi and I are on the same shift watch, so I'm stuck with his manic rants. I find listening to him rather than telling him to shut the fuck up is the lesser of two evils. Despite his seeming lack of intelligence, and the fact that he's an American, I do find him a generally likeable fellow. He's not as bad as I'm making him sound, I'm just venting here because that's what the writing is good for. He has good qualities too. I just can't think of any right now.

As I'm staring off the starboard side into the coast, Tobi sketches the Dusky Seaside Sparrow in one of his drawing books and shows it to me. Looks like any other bird to me. Tobi has this habit of providing unsolicited information about birds and their calls, but I listen because I'm interested in birds and made the mistake of letting him on to it. He said you could identify their calls by the CHIP-CHIP sound they made or WEE-WEE in short succession. Not anymore you can't. Why does he know the call of an extinct bird, anyway? That's an example of the kind of thing that happens with Tobi all the time.

We're approaching the equator. From the ship's perspective, it all looks like the same vast expanse of ocean planet. What changes is the light, the weather, the sea. For the past few days there's been relative calm seas, but pea soup fog that leaves us only fifty or sixty meters or so of visibility. Without radar and the computers this would be traveling blind, dead reckoning ourselves toward oblivion.

Yesterday afternoon we're at our shift change meeting, run exactly like we did things in Taos, and Tobi and Priya say we have to stop the ship and hit golf balls over the equator. They found an entire golf bag complete with clubs and balls in the closet adjacent the galley hall. Says it's a mariner's tradition and that we all need to do it. We're riding on I don't know how much enriched uranium powering this nuclear bomb of a deep-sea mining vessel, and these two are thinking of golf balls flying across the equator. I think that's great because it means the enormity of our situation is not really on their minds.

The seas have remained calm but everyone knows that won't last forever. What we're doing is kind of crazy, and the farther we go the more I get a sense of just how desperate this is. I'll get to the whole radio transmission. I just want to think about something else right now, like Taos and the desert. I miss the desert more than people, which is maybe a strange thing to feel. I also feel like I need to document some of those early days in Taos, just write it out. It's funny, when the thing is happening, when life is being lived, you never think to document it. But looking back you realize how fleeting everything is. That's just the way it is. We're living in history, and it moves like the current in this giant ocean, takes you with it. Taos was incredibly special times, and I'm realizing that now that it's gone, maybe forever.

If we make it alive out of all this, if Dead Man is to have his way, these writings of mine will become some kind of document of what happened. Committing this history to paper suggests the possibility of a future, so I continue this more out of some self-fulfilling prophecy than anything else. Some people just choose to see the hope in things. Others see the black. If you're reading this now, I guess it all worked out.

We're proof that people survived Virus (x). I alone wasn't proof of that. How many others survived the virus only to die alone at some point over the following decade? How many more Dead Mans were there in the desert that we just never found, never will? Who knows, maybe the survival rate was more than it seems, but how does one survive in this world truly alone?

I don't just mean that physically, but psychically, spiritually. I have spent a lot of time wondering how many of those initial survivors just didn't make it, and how easily I could have joined them. I didn't write this down at the time, but if you read this far, probably you could have guessed I was thinking about jumping off that bridge outside of Taos, ending my life at the Little Rio Grande below. I came so close to ending it right on the cusp of finding these people. I saw myself at the bottom of that canyon, dead, and saw the pleasure in escaping the reality of this life.

Everyone here had a trick to survival. I kept music going at almost all times, sometimes with words so I felt like I was hearing voices speak to me, and sometimes just classical synth-crush compositions, for the flow. Music just took me out of reality and onto another plane. It still helps. In Taos we listened to music together, and it took on a different reality when others were present. We were connected and the joy of that is something I can't fully describe. Medicine might be the best word for it.

Not to keep burying the lead, but I'm writing and revising these notes on a nuclear-powered United States deep-sea mining vessel on its way to the very edge of South America. Danh and Tobi got to Taos before the rest of us, and they worked together to get a solar-powered shortwave radio broadcast going. Tobi and Danh have lots in common, like they're both tech nerds and queer, so there's a whole other gay love story post-apocalyptic thread here that I'm sure the two of them would love for me to write out.

Tobi had a wife in his old life, and seemed to love her dearly, but they were the fluid types that maintained different relations, as was typical. I know more about Tobi's life than I asked to know. He has a sunny disposition which seems impossible in a world such as this. As with the others, I have no way of knowing what they were like before the virus.

The Tobi-Danh exploration for life on Earth was happening before I got there and they had been listening for a message, someone manning the station around the clock. It was quite ingenious and reflected such a strange sense of hope that I think they infected me with their belief in others still out there. Though they had a whole city to spread out, they made camp at an administrative building at the center of the historic old town, and the kitchen and the radio were built in the same room, with their stockpiles of food and supplies all under the same roof. I couldn't have planned it better myself. It meant that whoever was manning the radio was able to keep themselves busy with food prep and other tasks that could be completed in the main hall, complete with running water, a wood-burning stove, and solar cells that kept the lights on at night. The whole thing was mission oriented, which resonated with my constitution.

They even had enough juice from military-grade solar cells to run a small refrigerator and a food dehydrator, so they were always stockpiling food. One of them found a freeze-dried coffee cache, bless their souls, and we even had coffee. It was as civilized as it was going to get in Taos. They had covered the walls with woven rugs and artwork from the city, and at the center of the room was a large wooden table where we spent most of our time together, eating and talking and sometimes even laughing, finding joy in seeing each other together. I loved seeing other faces besides my own. Probably it's some deep evolutionary biology thing. The first thing we see in this world is a human face, and it's the one that loves us more than any other. We need to feel connected to stay alive. Survival is about getting back to your people. It's not meant to be a self-sustaining enterprise.

Tobi had managed to drag what appeared to be a priceless Georgia O'Keefe painting of a skull into the command center, and that hung on a large adobe wall opposite the windows. I love the painting and for some reason it had never occurred to me to make the world my oyster in that way. I think I preferred keeping my world small, intimate, just me. Tobi was a good counterbalance.

Just seeing other people, and the radio, though it hadn't produced a single lead, was a symbol of their vision for the future, that they believed as I did others were out there. I'm not going to lie. I actually liked these people. I saw them as virtuous which is sort of the last thing I think I'd say about anyone. But they were good people and I was one of them from the start. They brought out the best in me. Maybe any survivor would have done that, I don't know.

I was the last one to join the group, and we presumed others might pass through Taos like we all did and join our ranks, but years passed and no one came. Looking back, I would have to say those years were probably as good as I thought they could ever get. Is it a human flaw to always seek more? Or is that what makes us great? I guess they're not mutually exclusive impulses.

The Earth got a lot bigger after collapse and the virus. Somehow, we found each other and put our minds as one. One of the first expeditionary groups we sent was down to Roswell, and of course the Very Large Array, in the hopes that there was some easy answer to the sorrows of the world we had found ourselves surviving in. Contrary to the colorful conspiracy theories, which we all wished were true, New Mexico's version of Area 51 was just an empty military installation, not even an underground bunker, much less the remains of an alien life form. The only remains were the metal frames of stripped fighter jets and some experimental drone technologies, or so we guessed. The expedition brought back sketches and no one recognized them. Some of these drones looked very similar to what we operated in the war but I kept that to myself. Either way, may as well be oversized paperweights at this point. Some of those drawings are still up in our kitchen-radio command center, kind of souvenirs of the group's travels during those times.

When they got back from Roswell, Tobi was the most disappointed of anyone. He won't say it, but I know it has to do with his wife. Everyone has someone they carry with them, that visits them in dreams, talks to them. Tobi came back and explained his wedding band to us, maybe as a way to talk about her without talking about her. He said he saw a U.F.O once, it was black and shaped like a triangle. He flashed the ring, which was gold, and at its center was a large black onyx triangle. I had always noticed it but never bothered to ask. It just made sense on Tobi's finger. Tobi was a weird American, descended from hill people in Virginia or West Virginia, I will verify later where from. He said the U.F.O. came up at him, floated directly above his head, maybe a hundred meters, clear night, but moonlight so there was no mistaking the dark triangle in the silhouette. According to him, no drugs, no drinking, nothing, just the triangle out on the edge of the woods in the hills where he grew up.

And then he pulled this chain up from around his neck, kind of hidden beneath his sweat-stained yellow bandana he wore to protect his leathery skin from the sun, and on the chain was another ring, just like his, a little smaller. He said she wanted the same ring, even if she never saw it, and then he just started crying like I've never seen a grown man cry, not even some of the shit I saw on the Eastern Front. He just lost it and kept saying how much he missed her, snot running down his nose, it was a pathetic sight even if I was sympathetic.

I'm not going to lie, part of me still hated the Americans. In the war I killed people like Tobi without even blinking. At the time I would have said they deserved to die. North America is a landmine field because of the Americans. Now we were like family. That's not meant to be heartwarming. Fuck heartwarming, just a situational reality of being among the last living human beings on the planet. Friendship is a calculus based on survival, and that doesn't discount its legitimacy. It's biology, which precedes the relatively new invention of nationality.

When Tobi was done losing his shit, he tucked the ring back into his shirt, wiped away the tears and snot-hugged each one of us. That was one of the only times I ever heard him talk about his wife, and maybe the best thing to have come out of Roswell. At the time I remember thinking that New Mexico was starting to feel a lot smaller.

And the Very Large Array was still there, still as stone in the middle of the desert valley, offline and quiet as I imagined it to be. We each spoke of the experience with almost holy reverence. Danh and Maria stayed back in Taos in case anyone else was alive and well, found our Taos Safe signs and showed up looking for the lost colony of ours. Someone had to hold the fort. When we came back it seemed the three of us that went were moved by the experience, talking about how our people once searched for life in the universe. How grand and bold. Now we search for life on Earth, which was our worthy cause beyond anything before in human history.

In the back of my mind I was thinking we all had delusions of grandeur, but the more I thought about it, the more I realized what we were doing was in fact as important as the search for life in the universe once was. Maybe we really were the Neil Armstrongs, the Buzz Aldrins, the Yuri Gagarins, Alan Shepards, Valentina Tereshkovas, Sally Rides, Mae Jemisons, Aisha Khans, and Lina Zhengs of this world. These people were idolized in the California Republic. Hell, Neil Armstrong's face adorned the five-thousand-dollar bill. California led the world in space travel. We were the explorers, and fair to say it was the founding myth of the Republic that we were destined for the stars, the natural heirs to the former greatness of the United States.

I thought maybe in time and with increased exploration, we might find someone out there, or even a community. We still talk about another version of this world and finding a way to communicate with the colonists on the Moon and on Mars. Turns out the multinational corporations of the world, despite their destruction of Earth resources and interminable extraction, did something right, for themselves at least. Our people walk on Mars, and the dream would be to communicate with them once more. But they can't come back. Everyone knows that the light gravity on Mars becomes a permanent affair after you're there long enough. Earth gravity would crush their feeble bodies. The lunar colonies simulated Earth gravity so they could migrate back and forth at their leisure. Fuckers.

It's a fantasy of mine, getting to Mars, but I'm sure there's no way in hell they'd let us set foot on the Red Planet for fear of us bringing whatever disease or virus or whatever it was devoured Earth. That was a real problem before the virus, the danger of Earth microbes wreaking havoc on Mars with their immune systems adapted to a new world. Godspeed to the Martians, I really do wish them well. Turns out the unmen and other indentured workers on Mars are having the last laugh, masters of the solar system and all. There were some Marines up there with them. I take comfort in knowing some of my kin are roaming the red deserts making a home in the lava tubes beneath the Martian regolith.

The Moon colonists are another story entirely. Fuck 'em. I get heated just thinking about them. They have truly gotten away with murder and there's nothing any of us that's left can do about it. What's the word for the opposite of justice? Can someone tell me that? Probably a question for Dead Man with all his philosophical musings. And I bet it'd take him notebooks worth of ranting to come up with an answer. I keep thinking about that, because I don't know what that anti-justice word would be. Injustice is too week a word for what I'm thinking. Atrocity. Abomination. Something that invokes the cosmic scale of how fucked the situation is.

Whatever it is, that's exactly what the Moon fucks got, the exact opposite of justice. They live in the anti-torture chamber of their desires. Extracted pleasure. Most of the wealth of the Earth was in the hands of a few hundred people, half of whom were Californians, like California, Californians. Half of those people ended up on the Moon, the half that were vacationing at their lunar colony when the virus struck. The rest of us got the crumbs of civilization and the pleasure of watching their lives unfold on the threads that beamed back to Earth on the feed.

After collapse, some of these barons still had their own oil refineries and rocket launch systems hidden away on their private islands, mostly along the coast up in British Columbia and hidden away in the Salish Sea. These were some of the same people who developed the weapons-grade software that ran the mass coordinated drone strikes, or ran swarm algorithms on enemy databases with the intent of bringing them down, so is it any wonder that their private and personal industrial enterprises escaped the war unscathed? Drone warfare made a lot of rich people richer.

I mean, I got a lot of this through the feed, but there'd be reports of rogue rockets going up and no way that's happening off grid without their doing. You'd see reports of celebrities like William J. Longley, a.k.a. "Psycho Billy" up on the Moon doing a private country and western show for like twelve of these barons and it made me so sick to my stomach. The Earth was in ruins, absolute fucking ruins, people were herded to their deaths, bad, bad things happened, were happening, would continue to happen, and they were living in another world, not a make-believe one like we all got in the feed, a world of their own devising on the Moon. Flesh sex orgies full of disease-free fucks who didn't need the simstims for safe sex. These were the corporate barons who created the conditions of our peril. California Republic, U.S.A., the nation-state made no difference to them. They saw the entire human civilization project as a failed experiment and they were going to escape to the Moon and just watch the end of collapse from their lunar homes. Some people deserve to die, even still.

The worst of them by far was Noel Rodgers. He'd been stockpiling all of Earth's history on the Moon for decades, like actual books, and artwork, and grand pianos, and the car Bonnie and Clyde got shot in, whoever the fuck they were, weird shit like that, preparing for nuclear holocaust, or just the end of the long Anthropocene where he and his inner circle would live like kings on the Moon. He was like the ultimate corporate cult-leader and so many of the poor worshipped him for reasons beyond my understanding, though many of his own children had disowned him, refused to even talk to him.

Rodgers was like religion for the feeders, the ones who took everything they got from the feed and just accepted it as true. These people were the true architects of our demise, and if I could kill every last one of them, I think I would. I'm talking about justice here. Their infinite-wealth reality was a simulation of sorts almost worse than the feed. Their entire existence on the Moon was a simulacrum of life on Earth before collapse, like a 1950s fantasyland where everyone drove those big-ass cars, vibrant colors and red fins for fenders. Disneycorp sexcapade for the future. Stuff you'd see in the feed and think, wow, life seemed so pleasurable then. Hand me a cocktail and let's watch the doomsday clock tick to midnight. Must have been nice living out their Moon fantasies at everyone else's expense.

Entire cities in West Texas were erected to grow their food and other life support supplies, under the slogan, Space is for Everyone. Really? Space is for Everyone? You could say whatever you wanted in this world and people just went along with it. Whatever the opposite of justice is, that's what those Moon colonizers got. History really does belong to the victors. There is no justice. Punishment goes to those who least deserve it.

The ship is starting to rock quite a bit, rough seas and all this writing is making me feel sick. I think I'll call it a night and go get some fresh air on deck. Watching the ocean and the horizon line seems to put the stomach at ease. Looking out my porthole now and it looks like it's going to be a beautiful sunrise again today. The fog has given way to a sea of clouds above us, the blanket of despair lifted, letting a little light in on us. The Moon is out tonight lighting up the clouds in silver streaks. There are masses of birds, mostly Gulls all around us, streaking across the last of the night sky. We tried to stay in eyeshot of shore, away from the deep Atlantic waters, paralleling Florida, past Cuba and over towards the South American coast. The birds are coming in droves, so many that in some of their flocks they block out the moonlight like a cloud passing overhead.

Violence is not a choice.

Innovation fuels the engines of despair.

Your comfort sustains another's suffering.

Individuality is a dangerous illusion.

Clean air is a multispecies right.

A SLIVER OF A MESSAGE

IT'S FIFTY-FOUR DEGREES OUTSIDE. GETTING COOLER. Bright sun outside my stateroom and I think clear skies for the day ahead, which I'll be sleeping through. We're now more than halfway there, give or take. Bearing towards the edge of the South American continent. The plan is to just follow the coastline the whole way down. If we run into dangerous weather, we can head to shore and wait it out. So far it's been smooth sailing, well into winter in the northern hemisphere, past the threat of hurricanes. Tobi really does know how to run one of these things. There's a medical bay on the ship too and we've been getting our teeth cleaned this week by Maria, who was a dental hygienist before all this. Maria is probably even more useful to have around than Danh. Of all the people to survive, Maria is probably the one you would have picked, if you had a choice in the matter.

Were it not for her religiosity, I'd find her a lot more attractive. She seems content conversing with God. Who am I to judge given my strange proclivities? But with Danh being a medical doctor and Maria's dental expertise, I feel like I lucked out with the survivors I've found. Even Tobi, who I took to be kind of useless has proven to be worthy in guiding our ship across the ocean. Granted, he learned how to do this in a simulated environment via the feed. Priya deserves credit for being a hard worker. She led our farming efforts in Taos and has a background in horticulture. She's the youngest among us, late 20s.

Priya and I don't have much in common, but the sex is good if only because the options are limited. We appreciate each other's bodies far more than our personalities. What's wrong with that? One of the strange things about sex in the simstims was that it dehumanized the living breathing bodies we encountered out in the real world. I was reminded of that in my encounters with Priya. I wish I could say that there was no substitute for human touch, but that was the horror of the simstims. The boundaries between real life and the artificial encounters in the feed became indistinguishable. If that's not a damaging thing to our psyches, I don't know what is.

We five all have one meal together at our shift change, and we talk, laugh, find moments of joy in the time together. I'd say the shift changes are my favorite activity each day. Something to look forward to. Five of us together. We are survivors and an unlikely family. I could not have imagined a future such as this. We still talk about finding others, even if there is no one at Cabo San Pablo. Are we blindly optimistic? Maybe, but that might be out of necessity, to keep moving forward. Together. But after so many years in solitude, sometimes the feeling creeps in that I belong alone in this world. There's a strange comfort in that desire I can't explain, and it's something I don't like about myself.

Things change. On the timescales of our planet, radical transformation was part of our shared history. We recognized this and kept the faith even as we did the longhand math on the probability of finding other survivors. In the end, the math is ultimately on our side, insofar as there are others of you out there in the world. We're headed to the edge of South America on the prospect of such hopes, a sliver of a radio message that could be a profound waste of our time and energy. But our very existence serves as a kind of material evidence for our belief in you. Do you share that same faith in us?

The histories we share are all we have to offer to anyone we might find, and we recognize time as our greatest challenge. At the end of our life spans, the experiences that transformed human societies will exist only in the things we leave behind to tell the story. In my less depressed states I see the deep purpose and meaning behind these entries.

To communicate: to commune, to come together, to connect. A communion of people and ideas. To communicate is to survive. We see now it was profound inability for our people, our governments, our nations to communicate, and when that power was taken away from us, it was not Virus (x) or the endless ecological perils, it was the dissolution of a shared reality that brought about collapse. Therefore, above all else, we seek to communicate with you. To understand you, to commune. To be as one through shared understanding of language.

Also, I wish to recognize the origins of the word, broadcast, direct from the 1979 World Book Encyclopedia. Before the word had its connotations in communication it had its origins in agriculture, the literal beginnings of human civilization, in casting seeds across a fallow field.

And so yeah, we got a broadcast on our high-frequency radio. Something from South America. Middle of the night, almost midnight. Supposedly nighttime is the best time for these signals to bounce off the ionosphere, less ionospheric absorption. Like I said, Danh and Tobi were first-class nerds and had all this figured out. Keep the radio at the emergency band of 7.29 megahertz, send messages between dusk and dawn. More minds together have a better chance of solving problems. I would have not bothered with the radio when I was solo. But neither of them speaks Spanish. They would have been screwed without me and Maria.

We were able to translate what words came through the static, more or less immortalizing the message as the most important discovery of our collective lives together. We spent years in Taos. No one was coming, we felt as certain of that as was possible. And here was a beacon from South America, that a community was alive and calling for others to join. Despite our best efforts, we weren't able to transmit a message to the South Americans, at least not one that we got any confirmation that they'd received. Of the words that we could make out, I've made every attempt to get every line as close as possible to what I think we heard. We got one faint transmission. The first part of the message, probably a recording on loop came in the strongest and we agree on this:

Estamos aquí. Vivir juntos. Tenemos agricultura, alimentos, agua potable y niños. Estamos aquí en Cabo San Pablo.

We were certain on those words. People were living together in Cabo San Pablo, which we were able to figure out is on the very tip of South America. They had farming, food, clean water, and the thing we both heard and understood was children. They had kids there. When Maria and I heard that I remember each of us looking at each other wide-eyed and kind of arresting our brains for a moment. They were making babies in this world. I'll be goddamned. The rest of the message was mostly static, but we scratched out the best we could, and between the two of us, came up with this:

Greetings. If you are encountering this message, we wish you best prosperity and good will from Southern hemisphere. We wish to commune with you one day, to share our stories, and strengthen our mutual prosperities through every means available to us. We make our home in Cabo San Pablo, South American continent, where the [winds or weather?] bring hospitable conditions. Where do you call home? We welcome all visitors who cross the mountains or oceans to greet us. You will be welcomed warmly and with great joy.

And this, less clear:

We broadcast our message as far as . . . [unintelligible] . . . one of these messages will take root, that you will find it, and we can . . . [static], dear strangers/travelers who we hope one day to call our friends, even family. We await your response . . . [unintelligible]. Each morning we look to the horizon awaiting your arrival. Many generations we will wait, with much patience in our hearts, ready to welcome . . . [and then the message fades into static entirely].

There was elation, joy, and unanimous consent that we would journey to Cabo San Pablo as soon as we were ready. The two biggest reasons for us to make the trip, taking the great risk and upending our lives in Taos, beyond the obvious that there may be survivors down there, was the fact that they had children and agriculture. Both suggested a stability that we did not have in Taos. Our plan was hatched quickly. Make the trip across North America during the storm season and cross the oceans in late fall into early winter when it was safe to do so. And if the cross-continental trip took longer than expected, that was fine too, putting us at sea well after the threat of hurricanes had passed.

We could have farmed more heavily, and technically did grow some herbs and things, but we lived essentially as hunter-gatherers. Priya ran a greenhouse where we grew additional vegetables. The herds of elk, pronghorn, and mule deer meant we'd never go hungry. The mountains and forests surrounding Taos were teeming with life, to the point where you couldn't go out without a firearm capable of scaring off a bear or mountain lion, which we started to see at twilight and sunup with alarming regularity. Dying at the hands of one of these creatures, beautiful as they were, was an unacceptable proposition. When I say they were beautiful, again, kind of hard to put into words. You just had to be there to see their beautiful faces which seemed to mirror our own expressions of fear and loneliness.

In those years at Taos, the resurgence of life was undeniable. Surely the rest of the continent, and the world was seeing a rewilding of their environs. After collapse these changes started to become noticeable, with the air becoming cleaner and generally more breathable in industrial centers. And now with humans all but extinct, the five of us still wore masks but the filters were starting to last longer and longer. In the end, there was no question we were going to South America. We tried to get the signal to repeat, tried to reach them, but considered ourselves lucky to have even picked up their signal halfway around the world.

Two months later, we were staring out at the Atlantic Ocean, undocking and setting sail for Cabo San Pablo. Heading east rather than west allowed us to pass through the heart of the continent, but no signs of the living. The remnants of the civilized world were starting to show serious signs of decay. It was a spectacle to see. The world itself was undergoing a metamorphosis. The architectures of the old world were receding into nature, especially back east where the tropical lushness east of the Mississippi, along with the thick humidity made for a jungle-like encounter where anything that wasn't alive was getting overgrown and rotting into the ground. It reminded me of those pictures of South American ruins I found in the encyclopedia, long overgrown remnants of the once-great Inca civilization. This was the past manifesting itself in the future, my present. It did not feel real but there it was, America in ruins. No pyramids, but an endless stream of subdivisions, stripmalls, and intermittent urban centers transformed into jungles. The sound of the frogs after a rain was a chorus of delight that made me think I had missed out on years of life on the eastern side of the continent.

We also decided on east because Tobi had scouted out all these ships in the years he was exploring his side of the continent and he knew there were these nuclear-powered ships there that were perfectly operable. He'd even been on a few during his search for survivors, and took note that these vessels were still operable, powered up with relative ease. They were built to withstand end-of-world scenarios, and here we were. I'm sure these same kinds of ships were in place along the California coast, but it never occurred to me to search them. Ships in general terrified me, as does the ocean itself. We evolved out of the sea, not back into it. The desert reflected the kinds of internal states I was looking to foster in my mind and I owe what's left of my sanity to the desert.

It's not for nothing that the self-appointed captain of our ship learned how to drive one of these things from playing immersive feed simulations back in the day. He told us outright it was easy to disembark but that he seemed to have issues parking the ship at the dock. It takes a team to dock it and he expects us to figure it out. I tried to remind him none of us were mariners including him but reality doesn't dissuade someone like Tobi. I have serious concerns about us making it all the way down there and drowning at the edge of shore, our ship going down as it wrecks against the rocks.

Looking at the approach, the entire gambit is predicated on our ability to navigate some of the most dangerous waters on the planet. My vague recollections from the encyclopedia entries on the Strait of Magellan and Cape Horn invite dark thoughts about dying violent deaths at sea, what with impenetrable fog, forty-foot waves, the last icebergs breaking off from Antarctica, the convergence of massive ocean currents, and fierce winds that could overtake our ability to control the ship. I'll skip the freezing waters because we'd likely drown before the hypothermia could kill us.

Suffice to say this sailing is an act of desperation, but what does that even mean in a world such as this? We are decades past desperation, approaching something akin to delusion. But the message was real and what if there were others down there? Goddamnit, for all practical purposes we all died a decade ago with everyone else. The way I see it we're doing this on borrowed time. And if you want the real kicker, Tobi is from West Virginia, not Virginia, which is a world of difference. All this time I thought he might have at least some experience at sea but he's descended from Appalachian mountain folk, about as landlocked as you can get. I suppose if we do survive we'll have his feed simulations to thank for it. It's not lost on me I'm a Marine and should know something about the sea, but when was the last time the cavalry rode a fucking horse?

I can say with high probability that Tobi was partially insane before the virus and everything after. I don't joke around about this. I mean a lot of people were just plain crazy. People were fed a steady stream of horror stories, mostly true, and this led to paralyzing anxiety and paranoiac tendencies that surfaced in all kinds of abnormal behaviors. It was a symptom of living in the world as it was, being a feeder for so long. Reality itself was destabilized to such a degree that many people just lost their footing on parsing out facts from fiction. After the virus, all of us lost our sanity and had to claw it back over the next decade. I regularly have conversations with a dead man I never met. I am aware that's weird. The others assure me this is normal, and when I weigh my idiosyncrasies next to theirs, their point stands.

Maria says she talks to the Virgin Mary. I don't mean prayers to heaven. I mean full blown conversations with the mother of Jesus Christ, like what did you have for lunch and how-was-your-day type conversations. Her delusions are harmless, like mine, but it's fair to say that is old-world crazy. The central myths of these world religions were manifesting themselves in visual ways over the feed for a long time before the virus. Now, being detached from any kind of social reality, people like Maria who believed in these fictional characters as real-life entities were engaged in relationships with them.

Maybe these delusions kept her alive. To be honest, I was more sympathetic than not. What's normal in a situation like this?

Tobi is the one I worry about because I don't know what his tick is but he's sure as hell got one. No one goes this long alone after the virus and everything else and just keeps it together like nothing happened. How could one maintain the appearance of sanity in such a scenario unless they were already out of their minds? Weirdly, I think the current state of the world may have mellowed Tobi out. He and his wife were like doomsdayers and it's as if he half-expected this to happen.

His relationship with Danh also brings a measure of stability to not just them, but all of us, and makes us feel more like a family. Danh is so chill, and really a calculating individual. A perfect counterpoint to Tobi. Danh carries the twin burdens of surviving the Chinese incursion into Vietnam and his journey to the CR. Come to think of it, Danh is the only partial mariner among us. He crossed the Pacific as the last survivor in his family. The virus just makes his probability of his being alive all the more miraculous. He should be dead many times over, and yet here he stands.

Alright, gotta go. My turn to stand watch and make sure the coast is clear. There're no boats out here obviously, but it's part of the procedure, to keep an eye on the radar and WaMoS systems and make sure we're not running into anything. Once we get closer to Antarctica, there is the serious prospect of large ice chunks that have been breaking off the last few decades coming into our path, presuming they're not all melted already. And sea ice seems to be another danger. The large chunks could damage the hull but that's not a theory any of us cares to test. Dying by iceberg in a world like this would be an especially unacceptable death, worse even than the death by mountain lion scenario back in Taos.

It used to be humans were exploring our planet, and then they figured all that out, even the depths of the oceans. At the same time, we continued to study the planets, and the multinational corporations even got people to Mars, and a vacation colony for the corporate barons on the Moon. Is it bad that I hope those motherfuckers died horrible deaths? Some of those assholes are literal Nazis who believed in the superiority of the white race, and now they're on the Moon gloating in it, probably making white babies on the Moon. If there is a god, she needs to intervene on those assholes. But I digress. For the rest of us who couldn't get to the Moon or Mars, any hope for discovery, on Earth or otherwise, was an impossibility.

Well, that's just not true anymore is it? Me and the others are world explorers, on a mission of the highest order. We're maybe a week out now and depending on visibility can see the South American continent on our starboard side. We added a second person to keep watch for lights or other signs of life on the mainland, but thus far it's been a silent continent. We've even talked about embarking across the Atlantic to explore Africa, Europe, Asia one day. With the five of us, anything is possible. There are others out there. I believe it.

I do think it's clear to all of us that our lives carry profound significance for the future of our species. And not to remind myself of the obvious but putting all of us on a nuclear ship piloted by a frail-bodied hillbilly simulation nerd headed to South America seems like a crazy way to throw all our lives away. If these writings end up at the bottom of the Atlantic, it will be a loss for humanity. Who else is left to tell the story? That was Maria and Priya's argument anyway, more of a devil's advocate thing because I knew they really wanted to go too. After the message I almost instantly said fuck it, let's go. I was tired of riding bikes across the deserts of California waiting for a land mine to blow my legs off, me or one of the others vaporized in the desert. Since I came to Taos I've started to use reading glasses. My eyes are not as sharp as they used to be. What I'm saying is none of us is getting any younger and we needed a change of scenery and here was a literal invitation to Cabo San wherever-the-fuck to meet other people. We pulled out the maps and it couldn't be any further away. Tierra del Fuego. I'll take it. I'm writing these notes from my stateroom window sailing towards a strong impossibility, something dangerous and potentially life-threatening. What could be more human than this?

On a more personal note, our attempt at writing a history is perhaps more important to us as a form of therapy, sharing our stories both for ourselves and the implicit hope that someone, somewhere in the future, will read them. Except for Tobi who doesn't shut up, it was very difficult to get the group to talk about their experiences. But I think we all agreed the stories were important, and a way for us to bond. We are also an impromptu discussion group about our traumas, most of which honestly just doesn't get talked about much. Our energy and focus primarily goes to the future, to finding the things we need to live. But part of our survival depends on our healthy mental state, and we need to process this shit. If this doesn't make you laugh nothing will, but the others see me as the psychologist of the bunch because I listen to them. That's precisely how fucked we are.

Being on the ship has forced us to just sit and spend time together. We were always so busy on land, foraging, preparing, working with our hands, keeping busy and going about life as it was. The ship at sea may as well be headed to the Moon insofar as we are trapped together with no one but ourselves to keep us busy. The ship provides an introspection we've not yet experienced together.

Back in Taos, in the spring and fall, we'd travel the continent by bicycles. Mexico City. Vancouver, Atlanta, Boston. We've been to all those cities and dozens more, or should I say the periphery of the bombed-out ruins of those cities. But we didn't find a single sign of human life on any of those journeys. This doesn't discourage us entirely. If you do the math, finding someone in North America by random encounter has a very low probability of success, even if you both know you're looking for each other.

I used to lose my last girlfriend at the food & supply markets, and we both knew we were in there somewhere. I never mentioned her before because we broke up long before the virus. She wasn't a part of my life for a long time and I struggled with relationships. When the virus struck, we never even got a chance to reach out and talk. I should have reached out to her. Part of the experiences I've had in the past make me want to just retreat into myself. If you're reading this there's a lot more about me you don't know and never will. If the writing has taught me one thing it's that if there's any truth to any of this, it reveals itself in a structure of fiction. Reality is just too complex, which is probably why we invented stories in the first place.

Solitude at this scale asks you to question everything about yourself and your behaviors. Jadah was someone who cared for me. When I think about the list of people who loved me in this world, it's not so many people. I suppose it was always true that everything you ever loved in this world would go away eventually, along with yourself at some point. The virus compressed that reality into the span of a few weeks. I don't even remember the timespan. It just doesn't feel like it could have even been real, yet here we are. She had a laugh that made you smile. She was a counterpoint to my more introverted nature.

So all this time together on the ship I managed to get some formal interviews done with the group in increments, mostly after our meal together when there was less work left to do before our formal shift change. That midday meal was our window when we were all up together, night shift and day shift. I've edited the conversations together by individual and hope to add to these as I can. Putting them together I realize there's a side to these people that comes out in their words that changes my own perceptions of them. I feel like you can learn a lot about someone's inner thoughts through these in-depth conversations. I asked about things that would have never come up otherwise. You have to realize getting people to look back on things is hard, even when they're willing participants.

None of them has read what I've put together. Collectively, their stories are a history unto itself. My first project was to mark the period from the collapse to how we all met. I'm calling it Letters from Taos, because together, it was our first home. I hope we go back one day, hopefully with others. We're a community. I like everyone in it, most of the time. I tell myself the alternative, being alone in the world, is worse. Dead Man doesn't talk to me as much since I made contact with the others. Maybe he's gone for good. The others have brought me back to the land of the living.

And if my writing seems disjointed and out of order at times, or maybe goes on for too long here or there, fuck you. Mark Twain I am not. Shit, you probably don't even know who Mark Twain is. I'm a fucking scholar in this world. Ask me anything and I'll give you the answer right out of a 1979 in-the-flesh en-psyche-klo-pee-dee-ahh. I'm sure all those literary people had editors and proofreaders giving them feedback along the way, I've got only myself and I don't even want to go back and read what I wrote. What would be the point? This collection of writings is a conversation with myself and no one else.

If you're out there reading this one day, I hope you take something useful out of the history I present to you here, fragmented as it may be. Time accumulates in all sorts of ways. The breakdown of our bodies, or the collection of words that get put together brick by brick. What follows are the interviews with my fellow travelers. Letters from Taos, even though I put this together while sailing across the Atlantic Ocean.

LETTERS FROM TAOS

Tobi O'Neal, Point Pleasant, West Virginia

DON'T ASK ME WHAT HAPPENED. I don't know. Barely understand what happened to me and mine and even less out there. Maybe no one's going to ever know. Maybe there's some people, South Americans we're going to find, I don't know, maybe someone out there has all the answers. Wouldn't that be nice? This is no way to live, in the dark like this. I'm not too proud to say that had I not found you all, I don't know if I'd still be around.

Let me put it this way. Can you imagine what the survivors of Hiroshima or Nagasaki must have been thinking in the aftermath of those bombs, if you believe the feeds and that the U.S. actually dropped them in the first place? The survivors encountered an as-of-yet unexplained phenomenon, something that would have previously approached magic or science-fiction. Hand-of-god-biblical-end-of-the-world type situation. End of time.

Well, I feel like what we've experienced is something like what they might have experienced, only the events that transpired won't be made sense of by history. It's like the end of history and we're just here, observing things transpire.

Now what if the A-bomb consumed the world, and no one was left to tell the tale? Like the Japanese survivors just remained in that state of not-knowing. It comes to mind that we're living in a forever-world-of-not-knowing. No one is coming to place this thing, this virus, this plague of minds, this earthly ruin, whatever the heck we find ourselves in, no one is coming to explain things.

The depths of my sorrow are very fucking deep. Very dark depression. Very dark hole I fell into and yeah, I dug myself out. I made it here somehow, didn't I? I had nightmares from the start, still do, and the horrors in my sleep were something I wished I could have crawled back into rather than waking into a reality full of unspeakable dread. I know I'm preaching to the preacher here. You are alone in this world. Have a nice day. So yeah, post-virus solitude was a horror beyond measure.

The virus seems to not have affected lots of creatures, good for them. Maybe the virus is a kind of revenge on us humans. You talk about birds. Let me tell you I saw birds, from down in the hollers to the big cities, the likes of which I had never witnessed. I shit you not there were times when there were flocks of birds so big they were blocking out the sun.

Before all this I was a closet doomsdayer graymanning it all the way to Armageddon. The only one who knew the true measure of my madness was my wife. Roswell. She went along with it. Honestly, I'm not sure why. I think she just tolerated me because she loved me. She said we were compatible. I was a talker and she had a gift for listening, or just tuning me out. Her ability to tune me out and find something redeemable in my flawed persona was what made her special, and us "compatible." Not many other people could even stomach me much less spend their life with me.

I can't say her name, not to you, no offense. When I refer to her it's as Roswell, one of her nicknames. She believed in aliens and always wanted to make the trip to New Mexico. We never did. See where this is going? New Mexico had burnt to a crisp and been evacuated for years, supposedly one big landmine field. Again, all this was according to the feeds, who knew unless you lived in New Mexico, but we still wanted to make the trip out there. We had passports and could have made the crossing legally. The alien-anomalies thing was a point where our concentric circles overlapped.

After she died and years had gone by alone back east, I decided to make that trip to Roswell. Hopped on a bicycle and headed due west. It's fair to say my wife is the reason I'm still alive, and the reason I found you all. After Roswell, which really wasn't all that, just deserts and more of the same, I said a couple words for my wife out there in the deserts where she wanted to visit and started pedaling north. That's when I first saw one of Danh's signs: Taos Safe, and the rest, as they say, is history.

THEY WERE DRIVING AROUND IN THE NEIGHBORHOOD in a pickup truck, the bodies of three men tied to the back of the truck by ropes. Lord Jesus, they were dragging the bodies through the streets. I had seen these kinds of images in the feeds. To see this in my neighborhood, blood streaked across the street where our kids used to play. I didn't recognize the bodies, but I recognized the people in the truck, they were the husbands of some of my friends. Fellow *Mexicanos*. They were neighbors, lived a few streets over. That's when I remember having the conscious thought that there was no going back. If this was happening here, what was it like across the rest of the country? A few weeks later, everyone in the neighborhood was dead. It happened that fast. Is that how you remember it, *mija*?

In my memory of things, sometimes time moves very, very slowly, like seeing those bodies being dragged behind the truck or the men inside screaming. Other times I can honestly say the difference between two weeks and two months gets blurred. I was in some kind of daze or shock. I'd lost my family early on. God spared me for some grand design. Soon everything was quiet and there I was, alone in this world, shellshocked. It didn't go away. I lived as in a dream.

I buried my family in the backyard. During that period when everyone was burning the bodies, the smell got inside you, on your clothes, everything. The thought of it even now makes me sick. Near the end we were told to burn the bodies. Did they tell you the same? There is no forgetting. I'm telling you this now because you asked, and because I believe what you are doing is important.

I am a hopeful person, *mija*. I was raised to be grateful for the blessings bestowed upon us, whatever those may be, and to pray on the things that brought suffering, to have faith in Jesus Christ, *Gracia a Dios*. Deep down I hope future generations take some wisdom from all that transpired. I know you and the others would never think of it this way, but maybe Taos is the New Jerusalem. My faith in Jesus Christ kept me alive through all this. I just prayed and prayed, and the Lord gave me a sign. Here I am.

Digging those graves in the backyard was one long prayer, my back giving out and my body burning but I just kept saying "Lord please protect my children, Lord please protect my *Tomasito.*" He was a good man, a true servant of the Lord, loved our children, loved all the kids in the neighborhood. Up until the end, he was a hopeful man. The virus killed you before it took your life. I saw my husband dead before his physical body died. The sounds his body made stay with me.

Years went by, how many I do not know. A voice inside my head told me it was time to leave. My plan was to bike north looking for a sign. No one was coming to save me. So I prayed. I pedaled for days. I slept in the shade of the trees by day. The roads were barren, not like in those apocalypse streams where you see rows and rows of cars with skeletons in them. I got so tired of praying for the dead I just quit, God forgive me.

About a week into this, I trekked into a small town just north of us, Dalhart, Texas. We used to take the kids there once a year for the festivities. It was so quiet. There's a museum there about the Dust Bowl we took the kids to once, to educate them on the past, how things were and how things looked like they might be if we didn't prepare right for the future. That's when I first saw the sign. Taos Safe. I remember staring at the etching for a long time. Bright orange paint with black etched inside it. Was this real? Was Taos the answer I had been praying for? I said a prayer to our Lady of Guadalupe, asking her, did you send me this sign? And I remember thinking to myself, feet don't fail me now.

Finding you all has been a blessing, *mija. Gracias a Dios.* I pray we find the others in Cabo San Pablo. We have to explore. We have to continue searching. We have to find a future, or God willing, make one ourselves.

Priya Olaffsdotir, Eastern Colorado

I WAS BORN IN COLORADO, went to school there, worked on our family farm there. Compared to most I would say I had a privileged life, sort of in a bubble from a lot of what was going on around the world. My parents kept us off the feeds as much as they could, tried to instill in us a measure of critical thinking. They were educated farmers, they used to say, which was a joke I never fully understood as a kid. We were elevated, so the cooler temperatures didn't force relocation like it did for so many. Quite the opposite, our community grew a lot when I was a kid. The warming temperatures sort of made greenhouse farming a possibility year-round.

In those years I met other kids from Arizona, Utah, Montana, New Mexico, Oklahoma, and of course all over Central America. These kids' families were farmers too, or factory workers from some of those cities that succumbed to the heat and fires in the 70's. I think half of Phoenix must have relocated to Boulder, Fort Morgan, and the factory cities that were popping up everywhere.

Looking back those were hard times for all those families, but as a kid I didn't really understand the severity of things. A new kid shows up at school and we'd welcome them, become friends, play sports together. It didn't register with me that their families had lost everything and were coming to Fort Morgan out of necessity, basically with nothing.

After high school we worked in the fields together. California law made two years compulsory farming, regardless of education or training. Everyone had to eat, everyone had to work. Of course the Americans thought it was fascism or communism or whatever propaganda their swarm algorithms were spewing. They lived off the propaganda in the feeds. We lived off hydroponics, lots of soybeans and leafy greens.

There was always work in and around Fort Morgan, either as a farmer or later the radar parts manufacturing that piloted California's drone fleets. Looking back with some greater understanding of things, it's hard to believe the relatively hard times of the 70's would look rosy compared to what came. I have good memories of those times. It's strange to think all those people I knew died. Every one of them. Gone. They exist only in my memory. Those people deserved better. Each of us carries a world in our hearts. People deserve a life, and if nothing else, they deserve to be remembered.

My father was an immigrant. He knew how to farm in large industrial greenhouse systems and at the elevations we were at. It was similar to how Iceland produced their greenhouse vegetables, which they had been doing for generations thanks to geothermal heat and just the need to adapt to their particular region of the world.

Before I was born, my dad had to get his accreditations at the university where he met my mom. My mom's side of the family came from India around the turn of the century. They were a farming family and my grandparents taught agricultural courses at the university. Within a year of meeting my parents were married.

When my mom was pregnant with me, Bayer-Cargill collapsed and my dad was without work. My mom's side of the family helped them buy the family farm that me and my sisters were born in, and things worked out for my parents much better than they could have imagined, at least for a time. The collapse of the industrial agricultural industries opened up opportunities for families like mine who knew how to farm and could produce on a regional scale. It was an anarcho-communist cooperative model, and my dad taught a lot of the southwestern and Mexican immigrants the greenhouse methods Bayer-Cargill had hired him for. When the farmer's union was formed, the locals insisted my dad serve as the region's representative. And later, when he got sick, this was before the war, all those farmers who he had trained came to our family's aid.

I remember that fear of isolation and collapse because I lived it. I'm part of the first generation that grew up with collapse as part of our reality. We all lived it, but for us, it was for most of our lives. That's why it's important we talk, that we share the stories, and that you share them forward, if there's anyone out there to pass them onto. Back then, the threat of the collapse of industrial society seemed eminent. It was a decade without any sense of hope and it led to this. I don't think we wished it upon ourselves, not some self-fulfilling prophecy. All the wars had already been fought, all the decisions already made, we were just living through the aftermath and death throes of the civilized world. But why did the virus spare me?

Picking up on last night's conversation about end-of-world narratives. My father taught us a good deal about Icelandic history, as did my mother about our Indian identity. There's an Icelandic tale that really resonates with a lot we've talked about. The Icelanders were among the first to write down their stories, and I thought I'd mention that to you, given your interest on the subject. Like I've said, I'm really glad you're documenting our lives. You're doing that important work, being a knowledge bearer.

This was a story where a king, Gylfi, asks these three men on thrones a series of questions. Their names were Hár, Jafnhár, and Thridi, which translates to High, Just-as-High, and Third. The king who is himself disguised, asks them a bunch of questions, and at the end of the story, they disappear. Was it a trick-of-light from Odin? Nobody knows. I'm sure I won't get the story perfect, but it's better than nothing. The king asks about the beginning and the end of the world, and he gets this answer:

> *Ginnungagap, the great void before creation, was there, but grass nowhere.*
> *Next, Just-as-High said Niflheim was created many ages before the world was created.*
> *At its center was a spring called Vergelmir, roaring kettle.*
> *From it many rivers flow, including the river Gjöll, which lies next to Helgrind, the gates of hell.*
> *Third said, before there was a world in the southern region called Muspell, which means doomsday, it is bright and hot.*
> *Muspell flames and burns and is impassable to foreigners.*
> *Surtr, known as Black One, is the name of he who waits there at land's edge to defend it.*
> *Surtr has a flaming sword, and when the world ends, he will set off to battle and defeat all the gods, burning the whole world with fire.*
> *Surtr comes from the south, with the fiery destruction of branches.*
> *The sun shines from the sword of the goddess of the slain.*
> *Stone cliffs tumble and troll witches stumble.*
> *Men tread the road to hell as the sky splits apart.*

He steps back, the renowned son of earth, doomed from the
  serpent, fearing no shame.
  [The son of earth is Thor, by the way, killed by the sea serpent.]
The sun grows black, the earth sinks into the sea.
Steam surges up and the fire rages.
Heat reaches high against heaven itself.
Vigrid is the plain's name where Surtr and the dear gods
  meet in battle.
One hundred leagues it extends in each direction.
That field is destined for them.

Danh 'Dan' Hoàng, Chicago, Illinois

TELL YOU WHAT I KNOW. I know the problem with war, it never
ends. Everyone tell story of ending, peace talk, how you say, truce.
No war. Only story. War never end. Wars within wars. The dreams
of mothers, fathers, buried with them along the roads to every
village. This is true here, across countryside. Dreams buried in
ground. Bodies take dreams to grave. War inside each of us too.
Conflict eternal, inside us, manifests in globe, Earth war. Future
war. America always at war with itself.

I escape Vietnam through China. China powerful truth
bending machine. Aim of CCP surveillance all thoughts, create
algorithm to understand human machine, create one people with
one thought. Very ambitious mind control. China big power, big
nation, big idea, big control, big war with its people. Big rules. Too
many child, they kill child. Not enough child, they force child. Big
machine. Everyone have one thought. China occupies my people
for decades. Kill my family. Kill all my family. My family is gone
but I cannot talk about this. Chinese people die too. They die. War
never end. Future-war-forever-war. War eternal. War sickening
of human condition, uncurable.

My escape to British Columbia, to Chicago another story.
I cannot talk about this. Why do I live twice? I survive escape,
survive virus, survive everything. Why are we here today? Why
are we friends now? You hold my hand, I hold yours, we are one.
I should be dead many times.

I love you too. I see your pain, your beauty. I know you're a soldier, you tell no one, you say nothing, but I know. I know the look in eyes of soldier. It is inside you. Don't worry, your secret is safe with me.

One more thing. Thank you for listening. I look to stars sometimes, after everyone gone. Why I am still alive? No god for me, only question, why? I look to stars, see Firestar, we say Sao Hòa, wish the Martian Revolutionary victory. Our people live on Sao Hòa still. All people one people. No Earth virus in Mars. You understand this paradox? They take our philosophy to heart. New perspective on Firestar Planet. New beginning.

My heart on Mars. As the revolutionaries say, "war story your story."

Down here. They make new story. Story comes from the land. All story come from land. Always, everywhere. Mars people work together. Live together. Raise children together. Live and die together. We destined for stars, other planets, other worlds. I wish Martian revolutionary peace. We make new peace from our small people. Maybe people across ocean. I hope so.

I walk to Taos, long way. From Chicago. No bicycle just walking. You know I was medical doctor in Chicago. They need doctors and I try to help many people. Everyone die. Chicago big city. Hospital, we say no more patient, have to lock doors to hospital from inside. We cannot cure patient we have. Dead fill morgue on first day. One day! Can you imagine this? Dead all around us. In no time, city become very quiet. Burn bodies everywhere. Can you imagine a city on fire with its people? So many people on fire you feel the heat. All this happens in three weeks, maybe. Time stops, no one sleeps. It is not real for me.

Wintertime. The snow covers everything. Every car, road, everything. No footsteps. No path from car or bike. City asleep forever. Why I am alive? No answer but cold in city. I walk somewhere warm. I make plan to myself, leaving sign behind me, I go to Taos. How else I find others? Taos safe. Why not? Haha. Best way they come to me. Funny story how I create community.

One big accident. Why? Because I talk to universe, universe say to me, it cost nothing to dream. I dream us together in Taos. So I get to Taos, no one there, no problem, continue on. All the while make sign. Taos safe, Taos safe, Taos safe.

We have a saying in Vietnam, *not all storms bring destruction.* Well, this storm brings total destruction, almost. But new life too. Rain or wind maybe carry virus, but rain impregnate soil too, seeds grow, prairies grow over land mine. Animal fertilize plant. System grows healthy again. Not all storms bring destruction. Sometimes.

Love your oppressor; they know you.

The chains of society are invisible.

The lie of harmony is often sung in dissonance.

Distraction is a form of oppression.

Hallowed be the ruins of man.

THE WOMAN ON THE ROAD

One day a few years ago Danh and I were walking in the woods, on the edge of the mountains east of Taos where you could forage for mushrooms and berries, just get out and hear the birds in the forest. We were silent for maybe an hour, just walking and collecting berries along the footpath, and he starts with this story about walking the road.

He tells me he comes across a woman walking towards him on the desert road. He can't believe his eyes, thinks he is hallucinating, but sure enough the woman is real. He is overjoyed, smiling, says he begins to speak to her. She looks at him, appears to be listening, peering into his very soul. The two have found each other, they are not alone. They just stare at each other for what he says feels like an eternity, and then the woman speaks.

Have you seen my daughter?

She keeps asking, in the same concerned voice, have you seen my daughter? Danh stands there, thinks to himself, what do I say? He asks me what I would say. I just shrug at him, kind of enthralled by this story that he's never shared.

Sort of a big deal, another survivor in the world, you know? He says no one knows what they will do when faced with a mysterious question because there is no algorithm for chaos, not even in our complex, beautiful brains. Now Danh is repeating the question, like he's trapped in a memory loop and can't get out of the moment.

Have you seen my daughter, have you seen my daughter?

He asks her where she came from, how she survived. He tries to break through the mask of words. Each time she responds with the same answer: on a quest for her daughter obviously dead many years by this point. Danh stops asking her questions, he steps closer to the woman, puts out his hands, she reaches out to him. They touch. He says she is quite beautiful, and he can see the pain in her eyes. She asks for the last time:

Have you seen my daughter?

And then Danh stops picking berries, stops telling his story, looks up like a deer who has heard a noise in the woods, and he stares at me for what feels like a long time and now I'm wanting to hear how this story ends. He repeats what he says to the woman:

Can you describe her to me? What does she look like, what are her dreams?

Yes, he asks the lady in the desert these questions. If you knew Danh you would know he is capable of accepting other people's fictions as if they were true, because here is a man with actual love in his heart who sees the world as it is. Or maybe it's just that he's a doctor and he's used to broken people needing to be fixed.

Part of me wants to kill Danh, almost inexplicably, because his acceptance and even joy in the way he goes about living in this world infuriates me. But I listen, and in the end admire him for his strange courage, his sincere willingness to want to help people. There weren't many people like him when there were billions of us.

He continues. The woman describes her daughter, completely engages Danh's questions. Mind you, this woman has probably not seen another living human being for years. Where has this woman been? Where is she now? I ask Danh a million questions about how she survived, where she might have come from, what she was wearing, the color of her skin, he just ignores my questions and says the last thing he's going to say.

He says to the woman, as he points down the road from where he had just walked, where there was a small military outpost complete with even food reserves and water. He says, yes, I have seen the young woman you describe. I have spoken with her. We have shared our stories and she told me she is waiting for you. She is waiting for you there, at the military outpost. You must go see her. She told me to tell you to find her there, to make yourself at peace there, enjoying the clean water while she forages for berries in the woods.

There are no woods of course, he sounds just as delusional as the woman but I know he's just completing her fiction, trying to bring peace to her mind, this survivor. Who knows if the virus somehow affected her or if she just lost her mind. What if some of us got the dementia but never died? Who couldn't have lost their minds to this? Hell, there were plenty of Marines I served with who came home and did the only sane thing left to do and lost their shit. Suicide was a common occurrence for the Marines I served with. These were extremely normal responses to horrific experiences.

That was it.

We just kept picking berries, ascending the trail, listening to the wind. I looked over at Danh, after a very long silence, thinking about his story, and he looked back at me and just smiled. I had the same twin thoughts of loving and wanting to kill him in the same synapse. I had so many questions for Danh, but I thought on them knowing I would only get one answer out of him if I got any answer out of him at all. As we were walking together back to Taos, our satchels full of berries and mushrooms, I asked him if he ever went back looking for the woman.

Danh just looks over to me and without even breaking his stride he says, we can never go back.

Later, when I was by myself, I cried for that woman, alone somewhere out there, searching for a thing she was never going to find. It's impossible for anyone to be whole in this world, and maybe we're better off just disappeared. Danh's story convinced me. A person can be a ghost before they're a ghost. Sometimes it's better to just be a ghost, shed your life like a spent snakeskin. Evolve. We can never go back.

STANDING WATCH

LAST NIGHT DANH AND I WERE STANDING WATCH on the bridge, keeping our eyes fixed on the horizon for sea ice while Maria, Priya, and Tobi slept. They had spent the previous twenty-four hours navigating masses of ice floes as Tobi maintained our course towards Cabo San Pablo. We were in a relatively easy patch with good visibility beneath overcast skies. Danh got to telling another of his stories and I thought to write this one down before going to sleep. For some reason, Danh has shared more about his life within the last few weeks than the last five years. I think it's a side effect of staring out into the horizon. The blankness of the space evokes a rich inner life.

So Danh tells me in his early days of the virus when he was roaming the west writing his Taos Safe signs all over the place, that at one point he came across a field with a stand of flowers growing. They were called emperor's candlestick, and the flowers were in full bloom. He goes into detail describing the tall yellow flowers, which spire upwards and look like an illuminated candlestick, hence the name. The reason he's telling me this is because as he walked to the stand of flowers, maybe three meters high, he describes this buzzing sound getting louder in his ears, like many drones in the distance, and then he imitates the buzzing sound, which actually sounds a lot like the drone of the ship, same tone and everything. *Ooooohhhmmmm.* His hum tunes into the ship's hum and disappears into it.

When he got closer to the flowers, he saw hundreds of bees pollinating the yellow stalks. He stood there for a while watching the bees do their work. He said in Chicago bees were not present and he had thought they might even have gone extinct, that he wasn't sure. He had no idea how this giant stand of emperor's candlestick had found its way into the middle of nowhere. Maybe a bird dropped the seeds there a long time ago. He asks me like I would have any idea.

He said that he stayed there for seven days and seven nights while the bees worked sunup to sundown on the flowers. He described foraging for blackberries on the opposite side of the road, even getting a rare rain shower, but generally enjoying the shade of the large stand of flowers and the sound of the bees. When the bees had finished their work and left, Danh got up and continued walking in the direction he was headed. He said it almost with sadness in his voice, things got quiet again and I felt alone. The bees left, so I left. We each had our directions to move towards.

We had good times together that week, he says; I think he's talking to the bees, not me. Maybe the best week he can remember from the last decade. He's telling me all this as we stare out into relatively calm seas, moving in long cycles as if the ocean's surface was a large skin and a giant organism below was breathing. I'm not sure if he really stayed there for seven days or if it was some kind of metaphor about nature and observation. Come to think of it, I'm not even sure if it was a true story. The language barrier with Danh made it so sometimes I couldn't tell what he meant in the subtext of things. Like if he was making a joke, I often didn't get it because I was so focused on making sense of the syntax of his words. I'm sure he has similar thoughts about things I said.

But then when he was done talking about the bees, which he spoke about at great length and I presumed led towards some kind of conclusion, he just stared out the window of the bridge, sipping his tea. I thought this might have been one of those instances where I failed to comprehend a key point he had made, lost in the translation from his native tongue to his somewhat broken English. I waited a moment and then I said to him, what happened? Why did you stay there for seven days?

And you know what he says? He doesn't even look at me, he just keeps staring at the horizon as I'm wondering about the emperor's candlestick and the bees and Danh camped out by the road for a week, and he says without any intonation or meaning in his voice: no reason.

DUST STORM AT SEA

THIS IS NOT A RECOMMENDATION. *It is a mandate. You are bound by law to burn the bodies of the deceased. You are bound by law to burn the bodies of the deceased if they are in your domicile or if you come in contact with any deceased persons. You are bound by law to remain in your homes when not actively transporting or incinerating the bodies of the dead.*

Move the bodies of the deceased outside and burn them as soon as they are presumed dead. Do not wait until the next day, do not wait until morning. Do not wait until such time as you feel ready to burn the body, after family members have had time to mourn over the dead and spread the virus. The virus may be transmissible postmortem, therefore immediate cremation is essential. Do not wait. If you wait, you risk spreading the virus.

When handling the deceased, ensure minimal contact when transporting their bodies to the burn site. If you are in a city, do not transport bodies of the deceased down stairwells and do not use elevators. Do not move bodies into common spaces.

After wrapping in a blanket or sheet, remove the bodies out the nearest window and burn them in the streets. If you live in an area where a hole can be dug, it is recommended that you burn the bodies in a pit as deep as you can dig, at least three feet. If there is a designated burn site in your zone, you are bound by law to use it.

You are bound by law to wear respirators and gloves when carrying out the aforementioned duties and wash yourself afterwards with diluted bleach—one part bleach, to ten parts hot water—as hot as your skin allows. You are bound by law to incinerate the clothes, shoes, masks, eye protection, and gloves you wear after coming in contact with the dead. Do not delay. These hazardous materials can be transported in sealed plastic containers or trash bags. Burn soiled garments in the bags, do not remove them. Do not touch the dead. Do not go near the dead except to destroy their bodies by fire.

Do not touch the sick and dying. It is a violation of California law to come in direct physical contact with someone who exhibits symptoms of the virus. If necessary, assist the dying to designated burn sites while maintaining strict infection control protocols.

All deceased individuals are to be burned immediately. All deceased individuals are presumed to be infected. There are no exceptions to these executive orders. Your duties and responsibilities are to the living.

Follow the law. Protect the living. Do your civic duty. Our collective survival hinges on these actions. I believe I've been clear on your rights and responsibilities. At this time, your only right is to remain in your home. I am sharing these mandates by order of the President of California.

Are there any questions?

While I've done everything in my power not to think about what happened in that tiny window of time when all the world was dying and nothing anyone could do was going to stop it, I wake from the same nightmare which is really just a recurring memory of the last news conference in the CR, maybe ever, and it still comes to me in my dreams. It happened so fast, and now so long ago, but it lasts forever in my mind.

The seas were rough, throwing me around in my bunk, waking me up mid-nightmare. Rough seas are terrifying. Objectively speaking, your body is asking itself why the earth below your feet is giving out. I pulled back my bunk curtain and the wild colors of the sunset cast a strange pall over the room. It felt as if I was still in dreamworld. The jackets on the wall were moving like the hands of a broken clock.

A lot of my recent dreams take place in this world, the empty one, with only fragments of my old life creeping in. I've dreamed of Dead Man more too, faceless, wordless, but present. A few nights ago I was walking on the road. I saw a man on fire, screaming until he wasn't. I saw the husks of the airplanes outside Kanab. They started peeling away in the dust, like crumpled paper. I saw a spacecraft liftoff leaving its temporary scar across the sky.

And then my dad shows up in a wheelchair. He never used a wheelchair. He's dying from the virus and somehow I'm supposed to wheel him back on foot to Grizzly Flats. I'd never dreamed of my father before. It was one of those dread-type dreams where the task at hand is impossible. I couldn't save him. Couldn't save anyone.

I got dressed and headed out to the hall, rocking back and forth with the ship. I slid my hands along the railings to get to the stairway up to the bridge. With only the five of us this giant rig is so empty, and even then usually only two or three of us awake at the same time. Now more than ever I'm feeling trapped on this boat. Being at sea is the closest I've ever felt to being in prison or locked up in one of those goddamn shipping containers. The feeling of absolute helplessness that I imagine comes before death. I was ready to get to shore, back to earth and mud underfoot.

When I got to the bridge, Danh and Maria were standing together looking out with binoculars, wearing heavy-grade respirators. Visibility was poor. It was hazy out, like LA looked back in the day. This was the toxic dust that poured across the Atlantic from Africa and poisoned the eastern seaboards of North and South America. This was the dust full of not just heavy metals from decades of mining and pollution, but radioactive particles from the Nsuban Disaster in Ghana, when the plant there had a full meltdown. This was the dust that killed millions of Africans and probably contributed to the deaths of countless people on the American coasts. This was the murderous dust that penetrated the soil on the American continents and found its way into the bodies of every living thing, and into the flora that grew out of it.

To the east, a death cloud descended on us. To the west the sun glowed in strange hues I'd never seen before. The oceans around us were coming up in big walls of water. The clouds in the west lit up like long daggers that gave way into the negative space, the nothingness of the dust cloud. I'd never seen anything so dangerous create something so beautiful. It felt like the end of the world but I forgot that had already happened.

Maria said she saw the cloud coming in. It was doing strange things on the radar screens and then the winds came. The seas started picking up. She said it looked like a mountain in the clouds, coming down and blurring the horizon lines. There was no horizon line to the east. Sea state was getting ugly with green water coming up over the bow on some of the big dips we were making and cascading over the deck in giant walls of water. The ship would be fine, but this was knocking us around pretty good. I never heard our aluminum mugs clanking like this before from their hanging perches. The waves were rolling in from the east and we were more or less perpendicular to them, which made for some nasty rolls.

I told them I had to go and then went outside and puked off the side of the deck. That knocked me out for another twelve hours, holed up in my bunk. It felt like death. I was in a tranced non-sleeping state, and Dead Man kept knocking on my stateroom door. I never got up to check, but I know it was him, don't ask me why.

THE EASTERN FRONT

IT'S **CLEAR TO ME NO ONE IS GOING TO READ THIS** and if they do, just know that any true accounting of the time leading up to collapse and life before the virus is going to make them feel less human, less good about the nature of humanity. We all did bad things, or we were the survivors of bad things done to us. The whole history of our species is written by us for us, to justify our existence. We were the masters of our stories, telling ourselves we were advancing civilization as we did everything in our power to bring about extinction, not just for us, but a lot of other life on the planet.

We're fucked up creatures. We lie to ourselves as a matter of course. I am a fucked up human being. I did bad things, and they don't even measure up to the big picture. There is no morality that's going to justify the past, not mine, not anyone's. When I reread Dead Man's notes, it was like looking into a twisted mirror, the parts where he confessed his crimes, you know? Of course you don't. You're not real. I am writing to impossible ghosts in an impossible future.

How did Dead Man know I would find his notes and I would read them and they would reflect my own actions? Of the billions of people who died by virus, why was he one of a handful to survive and why find me? Why was he walking on Highway 59 in Arizona on a collision course with me? Why did we survive? Mother-fucking-fuck, another panic attack, I need to just scream again, get the phlegm out but it is inside me. It's the celluloid inside my skin that makes me real. What if the virus has me but is taking its time to destroy my mind before killing me? Putting words in my mouth, choking me out.

Desiccated motherfuck in the desert knew what was going to happen, in his life, somehow in mine, and just wrote it all down. Owned it.

I never told the others I was in the CRAF.

Served in a prison camp in Colorado.

Not even a hint.

My secret.

I lied through my silence so many times when I could have given myself away. Not far from Fort Morgan where Priya was from. I pretended to not know where it was as the pit of my stomach about fell out when she said the words: Fort Morgan. What are the odds? The universe conspires against us. Maybe there is a god really turning the screws on us. And maybe there's some justice there, letting her live to remind me of where I came from and what I did. Priya is a reminder of all the things I tried to forget about. Privileged fucking bitch living off the generational wealth of her family. That was California, California in a nutshell.

I never resisted.

Those Americans deserved to die.

I don't even think I allowed myself to engage the morality of my actions. I followed orders, like the Marine next to me and the Marine next to them. The handful who refused orders were shot on sight as traitors. What was I supposed to do? What were any of us supposed to do? Any attempts at old-world morality got yourself executed by your superiors, and where was the justice in suicide by morality? Morality conflicted with survival. Jane Ballard, survived.

Those Americans deserved to die. *We were you . . .*

I hosed out the ash and bones of the people who died holding onto their morality.

Those Americans deserved to die. . . . *And you will be us.*

The United States government had dropped millions of indictments from antiquated reaper drones, actual pamphlets that would rain down on us in the desert. We fucking burned these pamphlets by the millions. Wiped our asses with them. It was considered bad luck not to save the first paper leaflet that came down on you during your first days on the front. We quartered them neatly and slid them into the bottoms of our pockets, not wanting to be the one who didn't have a copy should one of your superior officers want to remind you why we were fighting an inherently evil enemy in the United States of America. The Americans had betrayed the constitution, betrayed the people, betrayed the bonds of affection that made the country more than just an imaginary community.

We wiped our ass with their bonds of affection.

For reasons that weren't always clear to me, I've carried that pamphlet with me ever since. Whatever I told myself about my actions in the war, the U.S. government made it abundantly clear that it wanted to imprison and kill all of us and do it legally through their Missouri murder court, which executed hundreds of thousands of CRAF and their families.

Fuck you and your drone-bomb indictments. Fuck you and your death squads. As far as the indictment was concerned, it was an invitation from the U.S. government to kill every American who supported these illegal executions of Californian citizens. The U.S. was in an unwinnable war but the top brass and the U.S. President, who may or may not have even been a real person, was sending every able-bodied American to the front.

All the truly advanced weaponry was on the west coast. We drone-bombed every American city into submission. The conspiracy about the U.S. president being a machine intelligence checks out when you think there was no scenario where the U.S. isn't defeated and yet they continued their military campaign. The U.S. killed those people, not us. Suicide by California.

We hated the Americans. There hadn't been a presidential election in fifteen years, and the east coast reigned with impunity. All this time shitholes like North and South Dakota, which housed all of fifteen backwoods cattle-fucking racist cowfuckers had twice as many senators as the strongest and most powerful economy on the planet: California. You take out those Moon colonizers who owned half the planet's resources and California still ran the engine of the global economy. A lot of people said California was the epicenter of the early feed, where a lot of the tech corporations behind the M.I. were working with the data mining contractors to make things seem more real. I believe it.

Everything was in California and we were being drained of our wealth at the expense of east coast states that were succumbing to the hurricanes and food shortages that destroyed the eastern seaboard, and expecting west-coast tax dollars to bail them out.

We kept the U.S. solvent for decades and got nothing in return. There was a hatred for eastern elites, pilfering our wealth with impunity and mocking us the entire time.

I remember an FNG asking me why we didn't have any U.S. prisoners of war, and I had to explain to her that we did, millions of them, and then I showed her the burn boxes and the ash pits. She puked and I laughed in her face. The next morning she was working alongside me cleaning out the ashes of the dead. All the U.S. had to do was surrender, and the killing would have stopped right then and there.

We executed them in large metal shipping containers simply left out in the sun. We baked them alive and burned the corpses in the metal boxes. You could tell how long they'd been cooking in there based on the screams and moans. It was like clockwork. I'd come in suited up in my silver heat suit looking like a goddamn astronaut with flamethrower in hand to clean up the mess. It was so hot. I drank liters of water on the hour, every hour.

After the bodies burnt out, we washed out the scorched remains with heavy-duty power hoses, the blackened corpses disintegrating into ash and bone under the heavy pressure. Bones were like paper and then they were nothing. Dust and mud. If it got on your boots the walking was heavy. Best to avoid the streams of the dead. Sometimes I laughed, don't ask me why.

The containers were all placed on hills to make the drainage easy, so what you got were these rivers of ash that cut into the packed desert floor. It was surreal looking, these narrow lines of black water and sludge caked and dried, curving elegantly down the hill, the different paths of watery ash crisscrossing and parting ways, all finding their way to the cesspools at the bottom of the hills. We'd bring in the next batch of prisoners, chained in a line, who were already half dead from cooking in the open sun, and they'd unwittingly be walking over the streams of the dead who preceded them. When you hosed out the ashes, the chains that bound them together washed clean, creating the sense that fire was magic. It was a disappearing act into the desert sand. The tide of suffering reduced to a puddle that dried quickly in the desert heat. People were reduced to dust, evaporated into nothing. I am sure we consumed some of their remains through our filtered masks. The filters clogged so easily in those shifts.

The sun would kill them just as well, but the metal containers took hours instead of days. If we had spare time after our shifts we'd sift through the ashes looking for any gold fillings and jewelry that made it through the screenings. They became a kind of currency amongst the Marines, not for their actual value, more the fetish value as in war trophies collected from the battlefield.

Worse than the death by slow burn, at night they poured diesel fuel in the cargo containers from vents up top and lit it up. The containers lit up at night were a spectacle of otherworldly horror and delight I cannot describe. You had to be there. Twenty-four hours a day. We worked in two twelve-hour shifts, noon to midnight, midnight to noon, so everybody got respite from the sun. In my mind, I'm still working the nightshift. I can't sleep in the dark anymore.

We never burned the babies. Any mother with a nursing child was separated out of the pens, given four walls and three square meals a day. The nursing mothers were spared. Pregnant women went into the fire. I'm not exactly sure why that's the way it was, but the babies never got incinerated. To tell the truth, I could never kill an infant like that. I'm glad those orders never came. I didn't feel good about burning the pregnant women but I did it. They were Americans and those babies were in the wrong fucking wombs. No, I haven't seen your fucking daughter. These were the same Americans who outlawed abortion. The same Americans who tried to enslave us, destroy us.

I know they were humans. But they weren't just any humans, they were Americans. And I burned plenty of people with skin as black as my own. It wasn't about race. We were way the fuck past that. It was about which side you were on, and if you were still American, you were on the side of dying, just that simple. We didn't kill those people. The U.S. government killed those people. If the United States had acknowledged the Republic, there would not have been a single drone launch the entire war. There would have been no war in the first place. Black, white, brown, no matter. You could have lived.

A lot of those prisoners were civilians that lived near the Californian borderlands. Sacramento Command wanted to clear out a zone on the U.S. side, so they'd have a buffer, and to send a message. The message was surrender or we're going to keep killing you. For every land mine the U.S. drones dropped and burrowed in our deserts, another hundred Americans would be killed. That was the official policy, not that anyone kept track of numbers. After a time, it was no longer enemy combatants, but any Americans we could round up to keep the machine going, to keep up with their drone bombing campaigns on the frontier. Like I said, they could have ended the war at any time. Suicide by California. This isn't a confession. It's a FUCK YOU!

I can't tell you how many American families we rounded up simply by telling them they would be given land and homes in Oklahoma or New Mexico if they surrendered, access to clean water. If one of them came up to me, begging, I told them everything would be fine, just follow the line, stay the course, everything will be A okay, you're in California now. Cry me a trail of fucking tears.

The U.S. doubled down with their drone strikes. We brought in more cargo containers. Oklahoma had already been destroyed by U.S. drone strikes, a dust cloud where prairies and farmlands once stood. Their drones seeded the land with cyanide grains so we couldn't raise cattle or do anything. Ever. It seemed like proper justice to offer these unwitting Americans a piece of the pie their tax dollars helped create.

Six million Californians were killed in Oklahoma City alone, and we lost all the oil refineries that remained after the famine of '72, notwithstanding the privately owned refineries that never made it to market. A lot of bioterrorism was happening then. That was the beginning of the legs coming out from under the table. The northern and western regions of Texas that seceded from the U.S. faced a similar fate. Millions dead. Phoenix holdouts, Los Alamos, Boulder, a host of military towns in the southwest and West Texas were annihilated.

The U.S. struck first and those attacks were never forgotten. Every American deserved to die after that. I never lost one day's sleep over burning them. They gave up their humanity. I got angry when the thunder and the storms came, because it meant we'd have to slow down or halt our operation. The hatred for the Americans was so great, no one thought twice about exterminating them. Hate is fuel. Hate is a weapon. It can keep you alive, give you a strength you never knew you had. The few Marines that resisted got themselves killed for no good fucking reason. We could have used their help.

I believe the CRAF would have killed every last American if Sacramento's demands weren't met, which was unconditional surrender. Add to those early U.S. attacks that trillions of dollars of California's wealthy elite were seized by the U.S. government, which meant that hundreds of thousands of workers were not going to be getting paid. California's declaration of war enabled those same unemployed to regain their pay by enlisting. That's what I did, and I would have done it either way. The U.S. claimed the bank seizures were legal as back taxes owed. The Republic wanted all of the funds returned, with eighty percent interest. The Republic's argument was that the war destabilized the already diminished U.S. dollar to such an extent that the American government would have to pay the difference or face the consequences.

Inside eighteen months we were pushing towards the Mississippi and probably would have crossed it by August of that year. U.S. currency was no longer the global currency, having plummeted against all the other major currencies in the world, not to mention all the decentralized currency that was flowing through the feed. The Europeans were supporting the U.S. war effort with loans and military equipment they knew they wouldn't get back. The Europeans had no intention of helping the U.S. win the war. They were giving just enough aid to allow the war to continue, for more Americans to be killed. They were sick fucks worse than us, just cowards. They wanted to see the empire that left them out to dry suffer a similar fate, but never lifted a finger against any of their aggressors. When I think of cowards and colonizers, I don't think of Americans first. I think of white-skinned Europeans. Skinny white men in suits making deals with the dead. Men on sinking ships. Men in parliamentary proceedings with those stupid fucking wigs. Men with their families being herded into those shipping containers in the desert.

Long economics story short, the Californian War for Independence was about breaking away from the failing dollar and the oppressors back east. Tens of millions of Americans died in the process. The death toll in the CRAF was felt mostly in the poor states, Indigenous in New Mexico and Arizona were nearly wiped out, Tejanos and poor whites in Idaho and Montana suffered heavy casualties. Oklahoma got it the worst. Oklahomans were practically extinct before the virus. Anyone who didn't evacuate the state after the first wave of U.S. attacks kissed their ass goodbye.

Back home, the State of California seemed to not even know there was a war going on. In San Francisco, L.A., Portland, and Seattle—life went on as usual while the rest of us died for their independence from U.S. oppression. I mean, the country was already divided long before the war, with all the wealth on the west coast. Atlanta, Charlotte, D.C, Baltimore, Philly, New York, Boston—have you ever been to those shitholes? They were on the verge of collapse before command bombed them back into the stone age. The joke was how do you know if you've hit your target in NYC? You don't.

New York was going underwater. California was mountainous. The cities just crept up into the hills and let the oceans come. We adapted. Had a plan. The palm trees in L.A. had no idea there was a crisis happening in the rest of the world. The sun shone and the beautiful people continued as planned, the wealthiest among them summering on the Moon's South Pole. Charmed lives while the rest of us were up to our eyeballs in the ash and the mud, sinews of muscle and blood, losing water weight in the endless heat. The U.S. increasingly taxed the west to hold the east together, and the Californians saw independence as a sure way to cut ties with the sinking dollar.

This wasn't information I got through the feeds. This was from conversations with Marines from these places. A lot of the Marines were defectors from the east, who in the first year of the war were offered their lives back if they swore an oath of allegiance to California and joined our ranks. We did in fact take prisoners in that first year, and I myself trained some of those defectors. These fuckers, mostly black and brown soldiers, enjoyed killing the Americans more than we did. They felt betrayed. They were betrayed, and California offered anyone willing to fight tax-free land on the reservations in the southwest, which was more than they had back east. We didn't tell them that land was as useless and inhospitable as it got. Just ask the dust.

After the war's escalation, every American soldier captured was killed on sight. No prisoners, no deals. But in those early days of the war, those American-turned-Californian Marines were from all over the country and could speak with authority about the things they were seeing with their own eyes back home. Some even had educations and advanced degrees. They were the poorest black and brown Americans who were the initial volunteers and seemed happy enough to join our ranks rather than being killed. I liked them.

I'm tired. I'm tired of all this shit. I'm tired of writing it out.

It's almost sunset and I've got to get some sleep before my deck watch. We're continuing to navigate the last of the Antarctic ice sheet that's broken off and following the current. It's a beautiful sight to see, even if it means all the ice is leaving the planet and we're the last living human beings to see it. I just hope the ice doesn't sink us. I think I saw an albatross yesterday. I remember reading they can stay in flight longer than most any other bird. I thought they'd be bigger.

STRANGE MESSAGES

I **HAD ANOTHER DREAM LAST NIGH**t, or a series of dreams maybe, and Dead Man was standing there, on the deck of the *Nerrivik*. I was on my night watch looking for icebergs and there he was. I heard his voice before I saw him standing there. In the dream, I kept looking for ice while he spoke.

And then I'm in the desert. I'm on the road and I'm coming up on this man in black who I later realize is Danh and he's asking me to describe my daughter and tells me to go to this abandoned cowboytown and wait for her there, gives me directions to the underground bunker. I tell this stranger in the desert that I didn't have the courage to burn the remains of my own family, does that make me a bad person, what I did? He doesn't respond, just looks at me.

I didn't have a daughter in Grizzly Flats, it was my parents that lived there. I was their daughter. We never burned the bodies of infant children. I didn't have a daughter so why would I be looking for one? The dream was reordering my life in strange ways. My mom asked about a woman named Angela. She said it with such conviction, but her mind was already gone at that point. If you saw my mom's eyes you would know something true that I could never put down in words. Could Angela have been the name of her granddaughter? I think it was the look in her eyes that made me doubt myself. My dad was in the wheelchair again, but that only existed in my dreams.

Have you seen my daughter?

I woke up from the nightmare because someone was knocking on my door. Three knocks.

What do you want?

Three more knocks, so I get up and Dead Man is at the door. He's continuing his rant, but since I'm awake now, he points as if to tell me to write this down, and then he whispers the following so as to not stir the others. I'm still dreaming but I'm awake this time. I'm possessed by this fucker:

Homo Sapiens have been at war with the Earth for some time now. Who do you think will win? Nuclear process procession: split the atom, draw out the power of a thousand suns, deep-seeded need to become one with the light, the telos to turn neutrons away, to degrade, alter the stability of a thing made whole, the purpose is to play the role Prometheus laid out, to play with fire, to split the atom, chain reaction, dig our own graves as in solitary slaves, Los Alamos families, scientists, sunglasses, pay grades, building a bomb in a city of half-lives, broken families, lost wives, husbands bear the lost costs of scientific exploration.

If splitting the atom invoked darkness, evolutionary biology would have prevented the threat of mutual destruction, nuclear holocaust, gamma radiation, unstable elements invading our bodies, the destruction of Earth systems' ability to sustain human life. It's the same reason children stare at prayers on the Fourth of July. It's the same reason . . . .

I stop writing, interrupt him, realizing I'm talking to a ghost, or the imagined ghost of a man whom I've never met, say to him, what are you talking about? Your brain got fried out there in the desert, man. It's funny, but I tended to forget he was an American. Why did I ignore that obvious fact? How quickly the imaginary boundaries of the nation states dissolved after there was no one left to share the mass delusions of social reality. With that logic, why did anyone have to die during the war? Humanity before nation states was a slogan I'd heard but it never saved anyone from the fire.

Dead-Man thinking was infecting my own thoughts. You don't think I don't know that? If I had found him in one of those shipping containers during the war, I'd have washed out his ashes along with everyone else's. That smell of flesh on fire seared into the brain. It made it so you couldn't eat. They weren't human, just screaming meat going up in smoke. Somehow, I think he knows what I've done, who I am and he's pissed. He doesn't skip a beat, so I write it all down, don't ask me why:

The cloud is a prayer preceding thought: a rain unsaid, a

particle in a series of nostalgic promises, a city in chains, sacred light enshrined in lies. The cloud is a piece of paper waiting to be sprouted, as the mathematician says, one scribbles some numbers and one may cause an explosion to occur.

Slow the fuck down, I say. He's going off, uninterrupted:

The cloud is a seed waiting for inscription, previously raindrop enshrined, an arrow of light, the color of movement, a stillness of perceptions, sacred being, supernatural. The cloud is a fog, a shrine of deceptions.

And then he pauses, I look up from my writing, stare at him for what must have been at least a minute, maybe longer. He comes closer, sits at the foot of the bed, hunched in beneath the top bunk and then he starts again, this time whispering his incoherent prayers as he puts his hand on my shoulder. Don't fucking touch me! I think this but refrain from speaking it out loud. Never give in on the delusions. I know this isn't real, it just feels that way. It happened so I'm writing it down.

One enters the secret city and finds no photographic evidence of its murderous past, as if to say, not guilty.

Is he talking about me, my own misdeeds in the war? I don't think so. They aren't even misdeeds. Dead Man isn't judgmental like that. I keep writing. His pace shortens. His voice rises above the hum of the ship, no longer a whisper. Someone is going to hear him. I'm going to be found out. Is this just me talking this out or is it in my head? How external do the delusions go?

The cloud is a Shapeshifter, beyond magic, beyond the realm of sensory data, endless transformation, endless transformation, endless transformation. We believe in God, we believe in borders, we believe in our Lord Jesus Christ, we believe in victory, we believe in God, we believe in killing, we believe in guns, we believe in bombs, war bonds. We believe in gods of our own devising, we believe in the power of language to dehumanize, we believe in our sacred scientists and the generals who guide them by holy hands made steady by god, rod, and gun.

We believe in the space race, white race, we believe in holy trinity, holy ghost ranch trinity, trinity of trinities: beginning middle and end trinity, birth life and death trinity, creator preserver destroyer trinity. One of the things uranium becomes when you bombard it with neutrons is Krypton, as in Superman Nietzsche Joel Siegel, trinity, comic book strip creating an illegal alien that we all worship, secretly, we desire to be that alien god, white skinned, able to move faster than a speeding bullet, Clark Kent, the reporter with x-ray vision, spaceflame into the sun leave this world behind, trinity, 1939.

I almost think to myself, how the fuck does Dead Man know my secret desires regarding Super Man, the old-world god, and then I realize he's just me, a character I made up because I'm too shy to speak my mind like this. He's like a comic book character, some two-bit alter ego I can't get out of my head. Am I the Clark Kent or the Superman in this relationship of ours? Which of us is the beard? And I'd been to all these places in the desert, of course:

Alamogordo, Camino Real, Jornada de Muerto, White Sands Wounded Knee Motel, Trinity site, holy Trinity, holy cannoli Trinity, drop the bomb and let's see Trinity, drop your pants and let's dance Trinity, reckless abandon Trinity, scientists have moral questions but only after unspeakable obscenity Trinity, war generals reflect on winning Trinity, zero sum games Trinity, war games Trinity, it's a bird no it's a plane birthing a bomb Trinity, soon we'll have body count and ecocide in Indochina Trinity, godless Trinity, you're a great American Trinity, one day we'll look back and say make America great again Trinity, you're standing on white sands Trinity.

There's a monument here, the sand was turned to radioactive glass, they call it trinitite, Trinity, nobody died yet Trinity, everyone died the war was raging in the minds of madmen Trinity, but now things have changed Trinity, radioactive decay being metaphor long lived for human evolution stalling out as downwinder DNA rifts apart due to unforeseen gamma rays Trinity, did you think of that Mister Oppenheimer, your genius genus and species Trinity, when you were arroganting your language-philosophy-science holy

Trinity, did you foresee disease x, that's it, Virus (x) has its roots in White Sands and Kyoto, Japan, did you think about problems outside your problems, did you reflect on the poems you translated Trinity?

What if this land wasn't your land, Trinity? What will you find splitting the atom, Trinity? Criticality describes conditions ideal for chain reaction, Trinity. A person place or thing. Trinity. Cargo containers, enflamed Trinity. Night skies enlightened, Trinity.

And then he takes a deep breath, lets go of my shoulder. I see his skinny hand which is desiccated like the hand in the desert I saw attached to the body of the wrinkled corpse. I think to rip his dried-up hand right off, but then I take comfort in knowing none of this is real. I can recover from this. Don't give the delusion more than it deserves by responding to it. Let it pass like the panic attacks. Hang onto the railings, it's why they're there. Try not to puke.

Dead Man keeps looking at me like he expects me to give him some response, some big thank-you-for-enlightening-me-with-your-bullshit kind of praise, but I just sit there and stare. I look at my watch and realize I still have an hour before my shift starts and I'm tired. I think of killing him right there, with my bare hands, but again put that thought to rest. He's weak and I'm strong but then I think to myself, you can't kill something that's already dead. I look away so he won't see the tears. And he says:

You consider the question, "what is the origin story of origin stories?" to be a distinctly scientific problem, don't you, Jane?

I start laughing, like I can't believe this is real, or maybe I was still crying. How does this ghost know my name? I know it's not real and yet here stands the specter of the desiccated fuck I wish I'd never saw or stooped down to search or know a single true thing about, and he knows my fucking name. There is power in naming, fuck him he knew that. He's just a ghost. He can leave anytime he wants, evaporate into thin air. I am trapped inside this skin. My flesh is sweating. I can't remember the last time I felt sweat like this on my skin. This is necessary. Just let it run its course.

Should have just kept walking. I realize now words are a virus, and this man plagued me bad. There is no earthly way I can get him or his words out of my head. There is no defense against the language of aggression and everything he spews at me is a weapon. But then I say to myself, like I wrote down: Jane Ballard. Survived. Can you get that through your thick skull? I grit my teeth like a fucking tiger and my eyeballs are so big they're going to pop out of my skull and I see he's a little scared. Chink in the armor.

And then he walks away, down the hall into the darkness. That's when I went back to bed and the next time there was a knock it was Priya telling me something was going on with Danh on the bridge, that he got a radio signal from Noel Rodgers on the Moon. I say, very plainly, too tired to express my disdain:

Fuck you, Priya, I'm trying to get some sleep before my shift.

She comes in, grabs me by the shoulders and I can see in her face she's not kidding. When I get to the bridge, still shaken by Dead Man's rant. Danh is on the radio, speaking in his broken English to what really does sound like Noel Rodgers, that arrogant mother fucker. This day is getting too weird. Sensorial overload. Something inside is breaking. I imagine the sound dried kindling makes when you splinter it into smaller sections. That's what's happening on my insides. I am flammable.

Honestly, I don't know what transpired in that conversation, and the more I think of it, I don't care. Great, so the people on the Moon are still alive, so it figures. I had always discounted them and took comfort in the fantasy that maybe they were dead, having cannibalized the last of each other, Noel Rodgers cooked up and shit out on the Moon. It wasn't to be that way. The stories don't go like you want them to. Why can't the stories just go like you want them to?

Danh said he recorded everything from the conversation, it was there in the ship's log, I could easily find it and include it in my notes but I'm just going to write down my impressions.

Who has time to go look up a fucking transcript? Anyway, it wouldn't do anything for the sense of urgency or hatred I had for this man who was still living in this universe of ours. No one else gets a transcript, why Rodgers? These notes are a transcript of my psychic dread, not a fucking transcript of events. So what if Noel Rodgers spoke to us at the end of the world? Christ on a cross it was just too much to handle.

I hear his voice filtered through the radio and he sounds scared which I love. I'm not awake yet, still rattled by Dead Man, but I focus in on the conversation. He's telling us the lunar workers up there are requesting, no demanding all kinds of things, rockets and food supplies and landing gear, and clearance codes for New Canaveral, and he breaks up but I swear I heard him say they cut his hand off when he was sleeping to get access to his private reserves, something to do with his fingerprint scan. It's too weird to make sense of. And we're all just listening and looking at each other and our faces are all saying the same exact thing: Noel Rodgers is alive. And what in the fuck is he talking about?

Danh speaks up first: what do we tell them?

Priya and Maria get in an argument about our responsibility to help these people, Priya taking the position that I do, fuck the Moonies.

Tobi is quiet for the first time since I can remember. I have no idea what he's thinking. I don't think Tobi has an idea what he's thinking half the time. I try not to hold it against him. He's American, it's not his fault.

Danh clicks on the receiver: *Mr. Rodgers! Hello! We are so happy. So happy to hear you are alive but how to help you we don't know. Many years we are down here on Earth. We find five of us. We are on ship at sea. No one help us.*

No response.

Maria says to ask how many people are alive up there and Danh follows suit:

Hello, Mr. Rodgers. How many people alive with you on Moon?

I just start laughing. This is so absurd I can't even believe it. Noel Rodgers alive on the Moon and asking Chicago Danh, one of five living human beings left on Earth, an immigrant MD from Vietnam, twice survived for help? Here is a portrait of desperation that gives me giddy pleasure. It sounds like Noel has no idea what's even happened down here which seems impossible. This guy owned every media company that existed and had his fingers in the pot of every world government. If he was alive he could have been surveillancing us with his proprietary satellites for years. Just when I think this world can't get any weirder, Noel Rodgers radios us from the Moon as we cross the South Atlantic surrounded by sea ice the size of Rhode Island for Christ's sake.

I haven't had time to process Dead Man's uninvited diatribe in my stateroom. As this conversation with the Moonies unfolds I think I see another albatross, or a seabird anyway, coast across the bow, almost at eyeline up here on the bridge. I look over and out the large glass windows. Dust storm long gone. We're surrounded by ice. Not good.

Rodgers continues:

Please. Just listen to me. Tell them the truth. That you are down there and can send all the things that they request. They are holding me hostage, you understand? They are not playing around up here. They are going to kill me. Do you understand me? Send them the codes already! If you can guarantee the supply ships they will let me go. I can't control them. Please, just send the supply ships.

Danh looks as confused as the rest of us, and without any explanation he responds: *Hi, Mr. Rodgers. We are not space travelers. We are just people. People alive on Earth.*

And then Rodgers cuts off but not before I hear a bunch of voices yelling in Arabic and we're all just standing there on the bridge and now the hum of the ship is what we're hearing and then Tobi says the first sensible thing I've heard him say in a long time.

It's great other people are alive. Wonderful, really. But they're all the way up there, and we're all the way down here. We're on different planetary bodies and on totally different wavelengths. We cannot help each other. Wish them well and tell them we'll try to keep in touch.

Two more birds coast by. They have to be albatrosses for no other reason than I want to see these birds. Add them to my imaginary bird counts. Before Maria and Priya start arguing, I say, I agree with Tobi, and head back to my stateroom to get some sleep. Dead Man has been doing a real number on my circadian rhythms and I need some sleep. Real shuteye. I can't say I share Tobi's elation that other people are alive, but it's a moot point, seeing as we're on different rocks and never shall the two meet. Whatever situation Noel Rodgers is trying to work out on the Moon, that's a problem for him and him alone.

THE DUSKY SEASIDE SPARROW PARADOX

The next day everyone was elated about the Moon talk, and yeah, I understood the deeper reasons and just kept my mouth shut, chewing on my protein brick and drinking my freeze-dried coffee which tasted like acid but it was warm. So people were alive on the Moon. So what? What were we supposed to do with that information? It was almost sad really, like they were marooned up there just like we were trapped here. At least we had the prospect of a life down here, maybe finding others. It wasn't a sustainable situation on the Moon. What a weird place to live. I guess if you have an endless supply of wealth you lose touch with what everyone else calls sensible. I guess I'm just in a deeply sad place right now. Learning of life on the Moon is opening up a wound that I've spent a decade trying to close.

I kept thinking about these dreams I'd been having and asking myself weird questions like what if the feed wasn't the worst thing that happened to us? What if our minds were the most dangerous part of the equation and Virus (x) was a kind of mercy killing? What if Noel Rodgers and his minions had exterminated humans on the planet so they could one day come back and repopulate it with their elitist white supremacist DNA? I couldn't figure out what the hell was going on up there with the Moon colonists and based on the conversations we had over meals together, the rest of us seemed to be perplexed about the situation. In a kind of paranoiac state as I was trying to fall asleep last night, I imagined Noel Rodgers from his Moon perch raining down a swarm drone strike on our location, just to make sure he'd wiped out the last remaining survivors. That was Amerinoid-level paranoia. I almost wished we hadn't responded to his radio message.

Danh tried to stay in contact with Noel, to no avail. Nothing but static. Danh tried to explain our situation down here but Rodgers seemed to want to hear none of it. What was the deeper meaning behind all this? What did Rodgers expect us to do for him down here? We were nobody. There were no clearance codes. Who did he think we were?

Frankly, these were the kinds of questions Dead Man would have asked, not me. The whole thing was pointless, horrifically depressing. The Moon transmission was a reminder that these extractors of the Earth's wealth were probably living their best lives in Shackleton Crater, and we were down here in the shit. Far as anyone left can tell, the human race had expired, been burnt in mass graves and buried for good. I was writing the obituary down here.

I was thinking about something Danh had once said about how our dreams end up in the graves with us. It made me think about how the Earth itself is where we end up, it's the downward turn, the nature of gravity, the body expired stills itself, someone digs the hole and we end up in it. In the meantime, enjoy walking the Earth, dust to dust and all that. Honestly, I was doing that best as I could. Fuck the Moon people. I finished my freeze-dried coffee and poured another cup. When I came out of my daydream they were still going on and on about Noel Rodgers survived on the fucking Moon.

Later, Maria told us Tobi said we were probably a few days from Cabo San Pablo, but that it could take longer due to all the ice we were having to navigate through. The ice was creating the most otherworldly abstract patterns out on the empty pallet of calm seas, but it was also fucking up our plans. There were shades of blue and grey against the white ice that I have never seen in my life, and I was drawn to them, could not look away even as I stood on the bow freezing as the sun set, leaning over the metal railings taking in the last ice as it made its way slowly north before eventually leaving the planet forever. Ice is a rock, or so it said in those encyclopedias back in Cowboytown. Everything has its melting point, its burning point, just a matter of degrees.

Those moments alone out with the sea ice might have been the most peaceful moments of my life, before or after the virus. I remember something a poet who survived Auschwitz once said:

"Even a crematorium can be made to look like a picture postcard," and when I see the ice floating away and what it means for the planet, my understanding deepens.

Back to reality. Did it concern no one that we were able to connect with people on the Moon but couldn't seem to connect by radio with the South Americans that had dragged us across the ocean and the other half of the world? You got the transmission from the Moon but not another sound from the South Americans? I didn't bother to bring that up. I'm certain we were all thinking the same thing.

It's not a question worth answering at this point. There was an old-world phrase that stuck in my mind, thinking it appropriate here: in for a penny, in for a pound. The history of human progress could probably best be summed up by that phrase. And then you find yourself stuck on a ship heading to the tip of South America, last among the survivors of a doomed species.

Acts of desperation are the best remedy for bouts with rational thought. Honestly, what else were we going to do? We didn't even talk about it. I have to believe they were all thinking the same thing and just kept pressing on. Honestly, people interested me less and less. Seeing the Earth and the life that was rebounding as a kind of tourist in South America was good enough for me. How were the Andes Condor populations doing down there? If they ate rats, I'm sure they're doing quite well.

This whole journey, if you want to call it that, was all about going out into the desert just to hear the music. I have to say, it worked. Looking back, those were the happiest days, or maybe I'd better say the least difficult days I'd had since before the virus. Being on the *Nerrivik* was causing some psychological problems for me, suffice to say. Not just the inability to go for walks and get out of town but the drone of the ship tortured me.

I'd been playing Bach over the loudspeakers and it helped but really just created more sonic noise. Not quite music. When I got to South America, I had the idea that I would just leave the group behind. They didn't need me and I didn't need them. What an interesting place to just start over again. Nothing personal. I liked them.

I thought about Priya. She and I had found some common ground, continued our relations on the ship from time to time, secret encounters in the relatively soundproof cocoon of the lifeboat. Maybe her and I could go. I needed someone younger around me to draw me back into the land of the living. Or maybe I'd just bike all the way back to Taos and meet them there if they ever went back. I wonder if anyone showed up and if they kept that Georgia O'Keefe skull painting on the wall. I loved seeing that painting every morning when I came into the command center to grab a cup of fresh freeze-dried coffee. It was almost living again.

Tobi generally sleeps when I'm awake and vice versa, but he leaves a report with his shift mate, Danh, who then reports to me, Priya, and Maria. Danh says if it gets much worse, he's saying we might just have to park it and wait for things to clear up, which he assures us they will. I don't bother asking how the fuck he would know anything about ice floes because I know it's just positive-thinking bullshit and not based in knowing anything.

The whole situation is not a problem in terms of food or supplies, but I'm not sure my final threads of sanity will hold that long. All this ice is being carried out with the currents and eventually melts. The good news about the sea ice is it has a calming effect on the seas, so I haven't been puking my guts out of late. On top of everything, I think I might be dehydrated, which is ironic considering we're not only a million miles from the desert but surrounded by water.

I'm not eating much either, don't ask me why. Priya asked me if I was okay which was alarming because Priya doesn't give a fuck about me, not really. I'm not sure how being on land again is going to help but I'm telling myself that it will. We weren't meant to live on the ocean or up on the Moon. We were meant to walk long distances and that's what I'd been doing more or less for the last decade and everything had been mostly fine. Maybe it was bicycling at night that kept me sane.

I had that dream again out in the desert where I'm floating above the creosotes and disembodied as the sun sets over the distant mountain range. I woke up thinking my bird fetish might have caused this whole flying above the Earth thing, but then my rational brain kicked in and I was reminded of the drones and the inherent danger of walking off the road in the desert. Think how insane our species is. We placed landmines in the Earth and made it dangerous to do the one thing we evolved better than any creature to do. Walk. I guess that gets at the reason why I fucking hate Noel Rodgers and the rest. They don't have to be down here in the shit.

Trying to stay positive. I keep telling myself I've always wanted to see the Andes mountains and the prospect of meeting these other survivors does mean something to me still, even if in the back of my mind I know no one is there. I've got my mind made up that I am going to start walking north, maybe go back to Grizzly Flats once more. Visit the spot where I buried my folks. Home is embedded in you. It's not where you're from, not the land itself, it's where you end up for the last time, where you bury your dead.

The good news is I don't think I'm a danger to anyone, myself or otherwise. I realize life is too precious in this world to hurt others. My biggest concern is Dead Man clearly visited me again last night, only this time I have no recollection of the encounter, no knock at my stateroom door, just these notes scribbled in my handwriting at the desk next to my bed. I think it's meant to be a prayer. Or a threat to my sanity. Maybe both. Like he's saying I am inside you, bitch. He's a nasty fucker. I would never write anything this stupid:

We believe in God, we believe in borders, we believe in our Lord Jesus Christ, we believe in victory, we believe in God, we believe in dehumanizing economic systems that lead us to this, we believe in killing, we believe in forcibly enlisting every god-fearing Californian Man, Woman and Nonbinary, we believe in guns, we believe in drone bombs, war bonds, we believe in the spirit of California and other abstract realities, we believe in the gods of our own devising, we believe in the power of language to dehumanize, we believe in our scientists, and the generals who guide them by holy hands made steady by god, rod, and gun,

Just as I finish reading this, I think it's time to just get rid of
all of this. Burn it in the ship's incinerator. I don't know how to
work it but I'm sure I can figure it out. The stuff is just becoming
too incriminating. If any of the others read this they'd think I'm
crazy as a Loon, and who knows what they'd do to me. Why do
birds get the reputation of being crazy? Maybe it's their screams?

Maria said she saw an albatross and I wish I would have seen
it just to see if it looked like the birds I previously saw, which I
want to say were albatrosses. There were twenty-one bird entries
under A alone in that encyclopedia. I counted, obviously. Albatross
was one, as was the Andean condor. Yeah, I was hoping to see one
of those in the flesh. Those fucking albatrosses are the metaphor
for all this I've been looking for.

Okay, I see it now, what's happening. It's on the next page, the one
I am writing right now, not as Jane Ballard or as Dead Man, but
as the amalgamation of the two, my true selves. Like the Sandhill
Crane tethered to Earth or the Sandhill Crane in flight, which I
used to think were two separate birds until I saw some of them
descend from flight back to Earth and realized those were the
same gray dino-birds with the red warpaint streaks on their faces.
Fucking beautiful, majestic birds. It just took the right moment to

figure out those two images in my head, of the terrestrial and aerial embodiment of these creatures were one and the same. I'm seeing that same metamorphosis of thought inside myself right now.

I think I've accepted the arguments of the extinction activists, HELP and the Spaceflamers and all the rest. Those fluorescent pamphlets worked their magic on me after all. Theirs was ultimately a critique of daily life. Theirs was a call to the failures of non-violence, a call for the cleansing fire, the reinvention of the understory, new life. You can't have story without understory. The forest floors of Earth are where the stories begin, like seeds cracking open, all at once rising up. Salvation. True resurrection. Life from the scorched Earth. Extinction really does lead to paradise. Those fuckers really had a vision! The Earth is more alive than ever. Dead Man was more a voice of reason than lunacy, and a bridge across the twin planes of my mind. That bridge to nowhere led to this moment.

We were once beautiful creatures that lost our minds to ideas, complex and insane conceptions of time. I can prove this here and now. Very easy. Our Earth calendar was started on the birth of the Messiah, the son of Man. Time was marked by the mass delusions of a species. But the Messiah is not a man. The Messiah is in the river below the bridge. The Messiah is in the parking lot. The Messiah is in the sky, taking winged flight en masse. The Messiah is in the High Plains deserts and in the forests east of Taos that dreams of you every night. The Messiah is in the sea ice outside my porthole, and in the depths of the sea. The Messiah is in the end of history, the end of ideas and human consciousness.

My hands are shaking. I'm hungry but haven't eaten anything in a while. I would do anything to take a walk right now. A real walk not this endless circle around the deck business. I mean a walk on the soft earth beneath my feed, I mean feet, not this metal ship. I munch on a green protein brick. It tastes like paper.

I look up from the notebook and see my pen knife, or rather, Dead Man's pen knife. The knife I have not taken out of my rucksack in what feels like years sits on the desk. The one with the two words inscribed in Mandarin Chinese on the sides. War trophy. Did Dead Man set it there as a warning or a prophecy? I'm envisioning blood on the exposed blade, but it's not mine. I'd forgotten I'd even had it. Never figured out what it said. I carried this thing around more as a memento of finding his desiccated corpse than as anything useful. Who needs a weapon in this world? Why is it out and why the dark thoughts?

I feel sick.

Dreams are dangerous things, I think to myself. The taste of bile comes up my throat and dances on my tongue. I'm having a lot of thoughts at the same time right now, another panic attack coming in waves over waves, like this is the big one that's going to sink my ship, stop my heart, rip that little pulsing muscle right out of my chest and watch me die right here. One of the thoughts that spurts out of my head in this orgy of synapses is the idea that I am Dead Man, that I dreamed up this whole story about a black girl from California, served in the CRAF just to escape my own histories. But that doesn't make any sense because I need an escape from myself, Jane Ballard. I don't even know the dead man's name. I mean, I named him Dead Man because he's an anonymous corpse in my life.

But why is there the thought of blood on an exposed blade and why is it my knife? These are questions that matter. They are the most important questions. Not this philosophical bullshit I've been writing about all this time. Why can't the dead stay dead? *What you are, that is what we were. What we are, that is what you will be.* I can still see that sign above the cemetery. What a privilege it was to die like a normal human being, be buried in an old-fashioned cemetery. We didn't know how good we had it.

As my throat sinks deeper into my chest, I have the thought once more that I should have never touched the body of that dead man in the desert, never read a single word he wrote, and how ironic that a dead man in the desert would be the thing to give me my own private virus. Why am I screaming at the top of my lungs right now? Why can't I catch my breath? I'd love a glass of water right now. My throat tastes like dust. Kill me and everyone else left in this world. I almost laugh at the thought that a dead man could be so dangerous, especially to someone like me. On the other hand, this world was built by dead men.

Jane Ballard. Survived.

There's still this creeping dread that I met Danh in the desert and there's a version of me hidden away somewhere that had a daughter, but that can't be the case, could it? Maybe I just wish for it to have been true. Even a bad fantasy would be better than the reality I'm finding myself in right now. I see why the feed was so attractive. Living in fictions was the way to go. I'd fuck a female wrestler-in-the-round right now.

The possibility of no future is closing in on me fast right now. I was happy out there in the desert reading my en-psyche-glow-pee-dee-ahhhs. Words soothed me. Stories soothed me. My story is not soothing me right now. Why am I even writing this down? I think it has to do with staying locked into this world, like looking at the world through a camera. Maybe it's not real as long as you keep your face attached to the eyepiece. It's just an image of the world. Now that sounds like something Dead Man would say. Little desiccated bitch.

Like clockwork I hear three knocks at the door but I don't bother to answer it. Everyone knows who it is as my throat sinks deeper into my gut. I'm going to puke now. I'm so thirsty. If I had a gun in my hand I'd probably kill myself and just be done with it. I never admitted it in these notes but that was the main reason for not carrying one. I never carried a gun and I never read Moby Dick. That shit was completely unreadable. I liked the first paragraph so I stole some of it. My grandmother was right. Brevity is a fucking virtue.

And now I'm moaning, like a death moan, it hurts so much. I'm moaning now as I write this. A curtain pulls back and I see things as they are, if only for a brief moment. I want to jump in the water just to get off this ship but the will to survive overrides the impulse. The image of the glowing orange sarcophagus comes into my mind. I need to get to the lifeboat. Jane Ballard. Jane Ballard. Jane Ballard. Survived. Godspeed to the others, but it's time for me to go. Too bad I had to figure that out on a ship navigating the Argentine Sea.

Bach's Violin Partita No.3 in E Major, Preludio is playing over the loudspeakers and I take a deep breath as the music washes over me, thinking who the fuck did that? *We were once you.* My throat is on fire. How long was I screaming. Could I get some water? *And you will be us.* How could I not have heard that until now? Ask me how I know the long-ass name of that track and I will tell you it's because I have probably heard it a hundred times on this ship, but I'm the one to play it, not them. Never them. It doesn't seem to get old. What does that say about us? There's no longer any emotion left in me, spent, the music merely serves as a mask over the industrial drone of the ship. *Ooohhhm.*

My moaning stops or I stop hearing it, not sure which. I can't breathe. I'm underwater, beneath the sea ice, waiting for the oxygen to run out and my brain to shut down. I realize just now the *Nerrivik's* drone was music too, ambient dark tones on long play, and maybe I should have spent more time listening to those sounds, like I had done by placing my ear on the railing in the stairwell of the focsle deck and listening to the deep ooohhhmm of the ship reverberating up and down the railings. Industrial musique concrete machine music.

Have you seen my daughter?

What a strange question to be asking at a time like this. And that's when I hear it and just scream everything out like this is the end of the world. The call of the Dusky Seaside Sparrow. That is the sound I've been hearing all these weeks. Is it a ghost of the bird, or Tobi fucking with me? I think I may have finally killed Tobi, or my body killed Tobi while it was possessed by a demon from the backroad desert highways of New Mexico or Utah or wherever the fuck. I almost get up to see if the bird is in the hallway but decide better of it. I wished I would have stepped on a land mine back then. It crossed my mind many times out in the night. Don't let the mind wield that kind of power over you. Don't let Dead Man know he's won. I should have never given him a name. I fucking told you there was power in naming.

I'm still screaming and it hurts my insides and I'm clutching my gut. Why do my eyes burn? I climb over the desk to look out the porthole and see the last slivers of sunlight setting over a frozen horizon. I can't drive this boat. How do I dock it if I ever find land again? I'm going to die at sea. We'll cross that bridge together if we ever get to it, me and Dead Man and the woman with the missing daughter if she's even real or just a story. But I suppose I can take her on too. The three of us beneath the skin. Everything is just a story. Ice surrounds the ship in the still waters and for the first time in a long time I am alone in the world.

BIRDS OF PARADISE

THE OCEAN IS BREATHING. I'm gliding over the rolling waves, sea spray stinging my face as my head sticks out the tiny hatch of the lifeboat. This is the closest I'm ever going to get to feeling what it's like to be a whale. After what seems like an eternity at sea, I'm trying to embrace the senseless beauty of the ocean, feel it on my skin because I know once I set foot on land I will never get on another ship as long as I live. Godspeed, dear *Nerrivik*. You could only take me so far.

The sea spray is freezing, and stings my cracked lips, but it feels good to breathe again. No mask as I take in the open air. The ocean mist clears the heavy metals and microtoxins and anyway at this point, fuck it. My solar pods are cranking William Basinski's *Cascade* as I ride the waves and it's sucking the fear right out of me.

I'm writing this from the enclosed cocoon of the orange sarcophagus, set to autopilot due west. Sometimes the best plan is the simplest one. Here I was needing saving from myself and this little orange glow-in-the-dark floating seedpod was the oversized pill I needed to swallow. Just a few hundred kilometers from land and this lifeboat can park itself right up on the beach and I'll be back on dry land again where I belong. I have no idea what the South American coast looks like, so if it's a bunch of cliff walls and rock ledges I'll cross that bridge when I get there.

Alone again for the first time in years, I already feel better. This dried protein brick actually tastes like chicken. And the watertight sarcophagus feels more like my subterranean pad back in Kanab than anything else. Or like a surrogate womb free-floating in the planet's belly waiting to birth me one last time onto dry land. Or going all the way back in our evolutionary history, like finding refuge in a cave, tucked away in the dark recesses, behind the fire, hoping the sabretooth tigers don't sniff us out. It's not lost on me that I'm headed to a place called Tierra del Fuego. Land of fire sort of sums everything up for me, like all of it. On a more positive note, if I see lights out on the coast when I get close, it will be history folding in on itself, an almost unimaginable symmetry to the fires Magellan saw six hundred years ago.

I might even have to drag this seedpod ashore and make an encampment out of it, spend a few months walking among the coastal seabirds, taking in the ecologies of the archipelago. Everything I need is in arm's reach down here, and a window in every direction. Whoever designed this vessel must have gotten inspiration from those big city hostels where each room is the size of an oversized coffin, you just climb in and go to sleep. By comparison this is cavernous. I can almost stand up straight without having to pop the hatch.

The seas are relatively calm which is maybe the final blessing I don't deserve but my insides are mostly untied and there's enough freeze-dried food and water to last me all the way to the coast. Before I strapped myself in and hit the high seas, I tied my bicycle real good onto the inside of the sarcophagus so I'm not alone in here. After all we'd been through I couldn't bring myself to leaving it on the *Nerrivik*.

By the way, for anyone out there reading this, it's the spring of 2101. This may be my real last entry so figured you might want something of a date to make sense of all this. It was spring when we left Massachusetts so doesn't that make it fall down here? The edge of South America seems like the perfect place to start a new accounting of things, forget the last decade of my lonely fucked up life, all the bad things I did and seem to continue to do.

Time to get a new bird count going. Year zero. I miss the birds more than anything and realize what I am is what I have been all along: the wannabe John Audubon of the apocalypse. If you don't know who that is, look him up in the en-sigh-glow-pee-dee-ahhh.

The sun is beginning to set. I pop my head out the hatch again to watch the light burn down to the end. The skies are clear, all the colors of the universe painted across the horizon. And then you're just standing there inside the orange pod listening to the waves crash against the hull thinking if this is how and where I die it was a hell of a run. Died with my bootstraps on. But there's no reason to get morbid it's just that a sunset is a tiny reminder of the finitude of things. Everything burns out, even the star at the center of all this. I wish I would have written more about the stars. After collapse, when the cities went dark, everyone looked to the night sky again. And after the virus, it was like the Earth had turned off the last lights and the universe could illuminate itself full throttle. You haven't lived until you see the Milky Way's scar cut across the night. The universe is a body of light. We're just in it for a brief moment. It feels good to know you're nothing, sort of takes the pressure off.

So humanity is gone for good, barring a few fuckers on the Moon, some Martian terraformers, and maybe a few Earthbound stragglers like me. So fucking what? In the grand scheme of deep time, what did any of this matter? The sunset and the lull of the rolling seas got my mind wandering across the cosmos, don't ask me why.

At the beginning of all this, on my initial return to Los Angeles, I saw the La Brea Tar Pits and thought of mastodons. I thought of you too and figured I could just leave your memory there in the black pits. The beginning is a black hole that goes back to a beginning further than we can know. There were so many birds overtaking the city, screaming endlessly. What were they trying to say to me?

The insect populations must have also gone wild as a result of our relative extinction. No more poisons to keep the insects and their diseased populations away from the cities. My guess is the birds have been feasting on the bugs and spreading like wildfire. Birds of Paradise. That's what all this seems like. Los Angeles, Taos, Cabo San Wherever-the-fuck and everywhere else belongs to the birds now. I am the chosen one. By fate or dumb luck, the fact remains I am the chosen one to herald the great birdrise on this planet.

The same resurgence must be happening out here at sea. What kinds of sea life were making a comeback beneath the surface? I'd seen massive schools of fish when we left Massachusetts and all through the Caribbean. It hadn't occurred to me at the time to note it because I was so transfixed on adapting to life on the *Nerrivik* and then losing my mind to Dead Man's invasive thoughts. I think of the word *fathom* and wonder if it has anything to do with the word *unfathomable*. Unmeasurable depths. Makes sense. Who knows what goes on down in the depths. I think of these words: subconscious, submerged, submarine, Marine, submachinegun, and back to subconscious, a little wordloop, but then I stop. This is the kind of thing Dead Man would do, not me.

It's dark out and I am listening to the sea, following the stars, waiting for land. The strobe atop the sarcophagus kicks on. For about the time it takes to blink, the night illuminates about ten yards out. Each flash and ten years go by, then one hundred, then a thousand. I was traveling back in time to a world that preceded humans. Another flash of the strobe. The sea spoke. Life was prospering on a young planet. Another flash, we were in the Cambrian explosion. Life was leaving the seas and making its way to land and eventually air. Another flash and then another. The mystery of the source of this water becomes clear. No one knows where the oceans came from. Forget about the virus, the origin of the sea is this planet's greatest mystery. Take comfort in the fact that it will never be solved.

And then I hear a bird and in an instant my mind snaps to the present moment. Birds are time's great miracle and they were waiting for me out here. I hadn't slept in twenty-four hours or more. This lifeboat was saving my life in more ways than one. This felt more like riding my bike across the desert than living like a machine on the *Nerrivik*. I climb below, lock the hatch, and munch on another protein brick before passing out.

I wake up and instinctively look out the eastward window. First light is coming up. I can't remember the last time I slept through the night. I keep checking the horizon and every time I keep seeing this long line of birds flying perpendicular to the boat. Endless. I think they're shearwaters but I'm not certain. They sound like they're being tortured, a long line of endless screams.

I check the compass and yes, they're headed north and I'm still going where I need to be. It's not lost on me that the sarcophagus is decades old and could crap out on me at any moment at which point I'm dead in the water. On the horizon, the ocean seems almost still and silent. The ice is long gone, probably less than a hundred kilometers from land if I had to guess.

And then I'm sleeping again, dreaming of the outskirts of San Diego where in my early days on the west coast I came across a bird sanctuary. This must have been ten years ago, almost exactly. San Diego was reduced to rubble but the suburbs were well outside the blast radius. The bird sanctuary was one of those places for educating schoolchildren and healing birds wounded by silent electric cars which always gave me a good laugh. The birds never heard it coming and BANG!

I parked the bike and walked in on the boardwalk to their large cages, planning to release a bunch of birds into the wild. I just wasn't thinking clearly. What I found instead were bunches of dead birds in locked cages. Later, riding back towards the interstate I started crying. Why was I sad about a couple dead birds? Why did I not feel the same thing for the human dead, back then or now? I think it may have something to do with mathematics or maybe it's my constitution. Maybe because it's strange to kill birds in captivity.

This wasn't a dream so much as a memory playing out as I was half asleep wondering what was real. If I die caged up on this lifeboat maybe some intelligent lifeform will find my corpse a few millennia from now, washed up on shore like some very fucked up message in a bottle.

It's midnight, I'm writing these notes in the dark as I approach the coast. It can't be far now, or my bearings were way off. Endless darkness out on the sea. I'm not worried because if I keep course due west I'll run into a continent, and if I die out here at sea then there's nothing to worry about.

On the *Nerrivik* there was the glow of the deck lights so it never felt like night. Here there is just the intermittent emergency strobe that flashes atop the sarcophagus, which is kind of funny considering there isn't anyone left on Earth to rescue me. But the black looks endless out there, like truly endless. I pop the hatch and just take in some of the cold air, feels good on my exposed skin.

I hear some birds out in the darkness and my heart skips a beat. Their calls are unknown. Why are they moving by night and where are they going? More and more birds. I'm getting close, like Christopher Columbus close, out here hearing signs of the New World. Birds are the ones who told those fuckers they weren't going to fall off the map. It was the birds that welcomed those madmen to the west. Their presence makes me feel as though I am not alone in this world.

Out in the distance, dead ahead due west, I swear to Christ I see some lights on the horizon. Like a string of beads flickering on a possible coastline. Not sure. Whatever it is, now is the time for dreaming, while the future is still pregnant with possibilities. The albatross come so close to the sarcophagus I think it's trying to commune with me. They are much bigger up close and in your face. I never mentioned how hard it is to get a sense of scale out at sea. Maybe I'm not done writing down these thoughts after all. Maybe I can start a new story, let Dead Man drown out here in the orange sarcophagus, locked up forever. Maybe that's how I kill him, light the fucker up with a flare inside the capsule and watch him burn for old time's sake, floating burn box like some Viking funeral. Got to pop the hatch so the fire can breathe again. Who will be left to wash out the ashes? The flare is gripped in my free hand and I've made my decision for Christ. This is it.

I pop the hatch, light the flare and fire it straight up into the night. Dead Man may have tried to kill me but he also saved my life, so we're even. All letters are love letters, even this one. If there's anyone out there I already know the first thing I'm going to say. And that's when I see them. Thousands of birds are flying across my field of vision, screaming in every direction. The albatross, the auk, the shearwaters, gulls, the spectacle of life in perpetual motion, moving with a single consciousness, guiding me home. The purple glow of the falling flare reflects off their glistening bodies as they knife through the dark and disappear into oblivion, but not before they remind me of the ties that bind. Animals are lost in this world, just like me.

NOTES

ACKNOWLEDGMENTS

Thanks to Jacob Blecher, Steve Brahlek, Lisa Danker Kreitzer, Matt Devine, Charles Tung, Josh Yates, Janneke Wade de-Jong, Nick Sambrato, and Scott Martin. Thank you to the editors of *Nunum* and *Trembling with Fear* for publishing the short stories that preceded this book. Special thanks to Phoebe Bosché and Paul Hunter.

BIOGRAPHICAL NOTES

Georg Koszulinski is an award-winning writer/director who has been producing films since 1999. His work spans a wide range of forms and styles, from feature-length narratives and social justice documentaries to short experimental films. His documentary work has enabled him to collaborate with a broad range of communities, including oceanographers and mariners studying climate change, Haida and Kwakwaka'wakw communities of the Pacific Northwest, migrant farmworkers in Florida, and Vodou practitioners in rural Haiti. Georg's forthcoming feature documentary *A Map of the World in Time*, filmed 34 days at sea in the Arctic Circle, was funded in part by the U.S. National Science Foundation and the European Geosciences Union, the latter awarding him the 2023 EGU Journalism Award. Georg recently wrote and directed the award-winning feature film, Red Earth (2023). The film won a juried prize at the Atlanta Film Festival, Best Feature Film at the New York Sci Fi Film Festival, and is available on a variety of streaming platforms. www.georgkoszulinski.com

Paul Hunter was a featured poet on *The News Hour* and has taught at the University of Washington, the Overlake School, the Skagit River Poetry Festival, and the Oregon Poetry Society. His first collection of farming poems, *Breaking Ground*, 2004, from Silverfish Review Press, was reviewed in *The New York Times*, and received the 2004 Washington State Book Award. Three companion volumes followed: *Ripening*, 2007, *Come the Harvest*, 2008, and *Stubble Field*, 2012. Davila Art & Books, Sisters, Oregon, published his book of prose poetry, *Clownery, In lieu of a life spent in harness*, 2017, and contemporary western novels *Sit a Tall Horse*, 2020 (2020 Will Rogers Medallion Award), *Mr. Brick & the Boys*, 2022, *Untaming the Valley*, 2024, and *Desert Crossing*, 2025.

Other Raven Books and Publications

Positively Uncivilized, essays by Rena Priest
  Paperback, ISBN 979-8-9914032-3-8
  eBook, ISBN 979-8-9914032-4-5

Treasures in Heaven, Raven 2nd edition, fiction by Kathleen Alcalá
  Paperback, ISBN 978-1-735480-6-7
  eBook, ISBN 979-8-9914032-0-7

This Light Called Darkness, A Raven Chronicles Anthology, Selected Work 1997–2005, Eds. Kathleen Alcalá, Phoebe Bosché, Paul Hunter, and Anna Odessa Linzer
  Paperback, ISBN 978-1-7354780-4-3

Poem of Stone and Bone: The Iconography of James W. Washington Jr. in Fourteen Stanzas and Thirty-One Days, by Carletta Carrington Wilson
  Paperback, ISBN 978-1-7354780-2-9

The Flower in the Skull, Raven 2nd edition, fiction by Kathleen Alcalá
  Paperback, ISBN 978-1-7354780-3-6
  eBook, ISBN 978-1-7354780-5-0

Words from the Café: An Anthology, Raven 2nd edition, edited by Anna Bálint, photographs by Willie J. Pugh
  Paperback, ISBN 978-0-9979468-9-5

Spirits of the Ordinary, A Tale of Casas Grandes, Raven 2nd edition, fiction by Kathleen Alcalá
  Paperback, ISBN 987-0-9979468-8-8
  eBook, ISBN 987-0-9979468-6-4

Take a Stand: Art Against Hate, A Raven Chronicles Anthology (Winner of the 2021 Washington State Book Award for Poetry), edited by Anna Bálint, Phoebe Bosché, and Thomas Hubbard
  Paperback, ISBN 978-0-9979468-7-1

Stealing Light, A Raven Chronicles Anthology, Selected Work 1991–1996, Edited by Kathleen Alcalá, Phoebe Bosché, Paul Hunter, and Stephanie Lawyer; Paperback, ISBN 978-0-9979468-5-7

Publisher's Ackowledgments

Raven is indebted to our 2025 Co-Sponsors for partial funding of our programs: the City of Seattle Office of Arts & Culture (Centering Arts & Racial Equity (C.A.R.E.); 4Culture (Sustained Support, through King County Lodging Tax and Doors Open funding). Thanks to all those who donated during the GIVE BIG 2025 Campaign for their generous donations in support of Raven publications and programs:

Crows: Kathleen Alcalá, Frances McCue
Steller's Jays: Susan Deer Cloud
Mockingbirds: Anonymous, Risa Denenberg, Sharon Hashimoto, Paul C. Hunter, Sibyl James, Larry Laurence, Joannie Stangeland, Harold Taw
Rooks: Lenora Good, Anna Linzer, John Mifsud, Mary Ellen Talley
Jackdaws: Rachel Beatty, Natalie Pascale Boisseau, Kathleen Flenniken, Diane Glancy, Sheryl Sirotnik
Magpies: Susan Pace

—Phoebe Bosché
Managing Editor, Raven Chronicles Press